DATE DUE

DEC 1 6 2004	
JUL 2 1 2005	
JUL 2 2007	

THE HAUNTING OF
GRANITE FALLS

~EVA IBBOTSON~

THE HAUNTING OF
Granite Falls

ILLUSTRATED BY KEVIN HAWKES

DUTTON CHILDREN'S BOOKS

NEW YORK

Copyright © 1987 by Eva Ibbotson
Illustrations copyright © 2004 by Kevin Hawkes

Library of Congress Cataloging-in-Publication Data
Ibbotson, Eva.
The haunting of Granite Falls / by Eva Ibbotson;
illustrated by Kevin Hawkes.—1st ed.
p. cm.
Summary: When twelve-year-old Alex's Scottish castle of Carra is sold, dismantled, and moved to Texas, the ghosts that raised him from a child have difficulty relocating.
ISBN 0-525-47192-8
[1. Ghosts—Fiction.   2. Orphans—Fiction.   3. People with disabilities—Fiction.   4. Kidnapping—Fiction.]
I. Hawkes, Kevin, ill. II. Title.
PZ7.I117Hau 2004
[Fic]—dc21   2003060669

Published in the United States 2004 by Dutton Children's Books,
a division of Penguin Young Readers Group
345 Hudson Street, New York, New York 10014
www.penguin.com

Originally published in Great Britain 1987
by Macmillan Children's Books, London
Typography by Jason Henry
Printed in USA   •   First American Edition
2 4 6 8 10 9 7 5 3 1

To Aaron and Irya
E.I.

THE HAUNTING OF GRANITE FALLS

ON A BLEAK and rocky spit of land that stretched like an arm into the gray North Sea stood the ancient castle of Carra.

There was no wilder or more lonely place in the whole of Scotland. Waves dashed themselves against Carra's grim towers; seabirds nested in the arrow slits on the ramparts; and on a stormy night the piled-up skulls in the gatehouse rattled together like billiard balls.

The castle had belonged to the MacBuffs of Carra for six hundred years and, as you would expect, they were a fierce and bloodthirsty lot. The first MacBuff had slaughtered a hundred rival clansmen, cut the hair from their heads, and woven it into a bell rope that he pulled when he wanted his servants to bring him his breakfast. The third MacBuff had thrown a dozen English prisoners into the dungeons and gone off on a fishing trip, leaving them to starve to death—and the wood on the drawbridge is stained to this day by the blood of the sixth MacBuff's relations: two aunts, a cousin, and a nephew, whom he simply murdered as they rode up to his house to spend Christmas.

But those times were past. The last few owners of Carra had been quite ordinary, though poor, and the time came when the castle and all its lands belonged to a twelve-year-old boy called Alex.

Alex's full name was Alexander Robert Hamilton MacBuff, laird of Carra, of Errenrig and Sethsay. He'd been six months old when his parents were drowned in a sailing accident, and since then he had lived at Carra with his great-aunt Geraldine, who had come to keep him company when he was left an orphan.

Alex had brown hair, which stood on end when he wasn't careful, and blue eyes that took everything in. He was a sensible and intelligent person, and he did his best to be a good master for Carra. But it wasn't easy, for there simply wasn't enough money to do what had to be done. Alex would be sitting at breakfast, and there'd be a loud splash outside the window. It would be a piece of the West Tower falling into the moat, greatly upsetting the frogs. Or he'd go up the wooden staircase to the gallery to fetch a book he needed for his homework and find that the top step just wasn't there—it had been eaten by deathwatch beetles. And everything got very dusty and dirty because there were only three servants where once there had been thirty: an old butler with a bad back, a housemaid with bad feet, and a cook who heard clunking noises in her head.

Alex did everything he could to save money. He bicycled each day to the Comprehensive School in Errenrig. He washed out his own jeans, and he helped with the housework. But a few months after his twelfth birthday, his accountant came with a lot of pieces of paper covered in figures, and when he had gone, Alex climbed onto the battlements and stood for a long time, looking out to sea.

Then he came down to find his aunt.

"I have thought and I have thought and I have thought," said Alex, "and I have decided that I simply have to sell the castle."

"I'm sure you're right, dear," replied Aunt Geraldine.

She was not upset, because she was not Scottish and she wanted to go and live somewhere warm like Torquay in a hotel with a Palm Court orchestra and kind waiters and a color TV in her bedroom.

So Alex wrote to the real-estate agents, and they came and put up a notice saying:

THIS CASTLE IS FOR SALE

After this, nothing happened for a long time. A few people came and asked stupid questions like, "Has it got central heating?" and went away again. Alex had almost given up hope of ever selling Carra when one day, as he was doing chemistry at school, the headmaster himself came into the lab. He told Alex to hurry home quickly because a Mr. Hiram C. Hopgood, an American millionaire, was coming to see the castle that very afternoon.

Alex just had time to change into his kilt (which the mice had eaten, but not badly) and hurry downstairs before Mr. Hopgood's big black car crossed the drawbridge and drew up in the courtyard.

Hiram Hopgood came from Texas, but he wasn't wearing a wide-brimmed hat, and he wasn't chewing gum or smoking a cigar. He was small, with a thin, clever face, tufty gray hair, and keen blue eyes behind gold-rimmed spectacles. Mr. Hopgood already had seventeen oil wells and three factories and a great many department stores, but now he had set his heart on a proper Scottish castle, which of course you cannot get in Texas, USA.

"You must be the laird himself," said Mr. Hopgood, coming to shake hands. Alex said yes he was, and began to show him around.

Mr. Hopgood seemed to be pleased with what he saw. He liked the West Tower with its screech owls and clusters of sleeping bats, and he liked the East Tower with its rusty thumbscrews and the iron collars for squeezing people's throats. He liked the underground passages and the well, with its dark and slimy water; and most of all he liked the bloodstained drawbridge and the bell rope woven from the hair of a hundred slaughtered MacCarpetdales.

When they had finished, Alex took him to have tea with his aunt Geraldine, and then he and Mr. Hopgood went into the library to do business.

"I don't mind telling you, Alex," said Mr. Hopgood, "that I like this castle. I like it very much. It's natural. It's unspoiled. It's Scottish to the backbone."

Just to show how unspoiled everything was, two large cockroaches walked slowly across the floor and stopped by Mr. Hopgood's shoe, but he didn't seem to mind in the least.

"If I want hygiene and sanitation, I can find it in Texas," he said. "But what I want is atmosphere. And atmosphere is what Carra has got. Now mind you, I've got to check out a few points first . . . take a few measurements . . . get a few experts. But I don't let experts push me around, and I'm pretty certain that Carra's what I'm looking for."

Alex tried not to look too pleased, because he knew

that when one is doing business one must keep cool, but his eyes as he stared at Mr. Hopgood were full of hope, for he could see that the American would be a good master for his home.

"Your accountant tells me you want to hang on to that little island out there. Sethsay. Is that right?"

"Yes, sir. It's got a small farm on the far side. I'd like to live there when I'm old."

Mr. Hopgood nodded. "Fair enough. I've no use for the island. It's the castle I want. As you know, it's in a pretty ropy condition, so all I'm prepared to offer is half a million. Pounds, of course, not dollars. Five hundred thousand pounds."

Alex blinked, but he did not bother to pinch himself to see if he was awake. Being awake and being asleep are quite different, he had found. Half a million pounds! Enough to give all the servants what they needed for their old age, keep Aunt Geraldine in a grand hotel, and still have plenty left over for the journeys he meant to make as soon as he was old enough. Enough to go to Patagonia and look for the giant sloth . . . Enough to go to the Himalayas and find a yeti . . .

"I'll have to see your lawyers, of course," Mr. Hopgood went on, "but as far as you're concerned, would that be acceptable?"

"Yes, sir. Absolutely. It would be fine."

Mr. Hopgood took a peppermint out of a paper bag and offered one to Alex.

"There's just one thing," he said. "A very important thing indeed. I will buy your castle—*but only if there are no ghosts!*"

Alex swallowed. "I thought Americans always wanted ghosts? I thought they liked everything that was old?"

"Well, I don't. Personally, I don't mind one way or the other. Ghosts or no ghosts, it's all the same to me. But I've got a little daughter and she's delicate. She got polio when she was small. My wife didn't believe in vaccines and . . . well, there you are. She's ten now; one foot drags a bit, but she might grow out of it, the doctors say. Only, of course, she's got to be careful—she mustn't have any shocks. Would you like to see her picture?"

He took out a photograph and handed it to Alex. From the way he looked at it, Alex could see that he loved his daughter very much. "Her name's Helen," said Mr. Hopgood, "and she's nobody's fool."

Alex had expected to see a girl in a party dress with blond curls, perhaps, holding a teddy bear and smiling like a girl in an advertisement. But Helen wasn't smiling. Her head rested on her hands and her dark straight hair fell over her fingers. She had a thin face and brown eyes and looked serious, as though she was thinking something out.

"Her mother's dead and I guess I spoil her. But that business of no shocks is for real. So you must give me your word of honor that Carra Castle has no ghosts. If you can do that, the deal goes through."

It was one of the most difficult moments of Alex's life. For a full minute, he couldn't speak at all. Then he said, "How soon would you want the castle, Mr. Hopgood?"

"Well, the end of June, I reckon. I'd expect to take possession on the first of July."

Alex looked him straight in the eyes. Then he said: "I swear to you, sir, that the castle you'll be buying will be entirely free of ghosts."

THE FOLLOWING MORNING Alex went to have a word with his aunt Geraldine and told her what he meant to do. Then he pulled the bell rope made from the hair of a hundred MacCarpetdales. In the old days this would have meant that the servants were to come to the master of the house. Now it meant that Alex was on the way to the kitchen.

"As you'll have heard," said Alex to his staff, "Mr. Hopgood wants to buy the castle. If he buys it, I'll give each of you fifteen thousand pounds because you have worked so hard."

"Fifteen thousand pounds! Well, I never!" Cook was quite pink with pleasure.

"But Mr. Hopgood has made one condition. He will only buy Carra if there are no ghosts."

The faces of the three servants fell. "Well, that's that,

then, isn't it," said the butler miserably. He'd been looking forward so much to joining his brother in Canada.

"Nothing more to be said then, is there?" said the housemaid with a sniff.

"Yes, there is." Alex's voice was strong and confident, and it was hard to believe that he was only twelve years old. "By the time Mr. Hopgood comes to live in the castle, there won't be a ghost in the place."

The servants stared at him. "What are you going to do?" asked the butler. "You'll not be going to exorcise them, surely?"

Alex shook his head. "No. That would be too cruel. I'm going to appeal to their better nature." And seeing that the housemaid did not understand what he meant, he said, "I'm going to ask them to be noble and go somewhere else. To be unselfish. Ghosts *can* be unselfish, I'm sure of it. Only you must promise me not to tell anyone who comes that Carra was once haunted."

The servants promised—but when Alex had gone they shook their heads.

"Noble, indeed!" said the butler. "Unselfish! That lot of wailers! They'll never budge. Exorcism is the only thing to shift them, and Master Alex is too softhearted. Why, he's proper daft about them, specially that dratted dog."

Alex himself was not as hopeful as he had pretended. But he had given his word to Mr. Hopgood, so as soon as midnight struck and the bats had fluttered out to feed, he climbed to the top of the East Tower, sat down on an old chest, and waited.

He did not have to wait for long. Alex's ghosts always knew when he was near. A sinister dark vapor crept through the room and it became very cold. Then a filmy, wavering blob of ectoplasm appeared . . . became clearer . . . became properly visible—and Krok the Viking stood before Alex.

"Greetings, O Laird of Carra," boomed the warrior, rubbing his enormous hairy stomach where the chain shirt tickled him.

He was a huge ghost, six feet four in his thonged sandals, with a thick, curly beard that had been red when he was alive, and now was home to many of the wood lice and beetles who lived in the castle.

"Greetings, Krok Fullbelly," said Alex politely, and sighed, for the news he was bringing lay like a weight against his chest.

Krok had haunted Carra when the castle was just a fort built to defend Britain from the Northmen. Fullbelly the Fearless they'd called him, and he'd been a brave and mighty soldier, leaping ashore from his longboat and burning, pillaging, and slaying with the best of them.

But one day, as he was pulling a captive woman out of her burning hut and dragging her toward his ship, he suddenly said, "Enough! I'm not going on any more raids. After this I'm staying at home."

It wasn't the fighting Krok minded—over the years he'd lost an ear, three of his hairy toes, and his right thumb and hardly noticed, because Vikings are like that. It was taking all those screaming women back that upset him. The way they kicked and shrieked and bit—and then when he got them back home, the way they lay about in his house, gossiping and having babies.

But of course if you are a Viking you cannot say, "Enough!" and get away with it. The king, who was called Harald Hardnose, ordered Krok to be put to death then and there, and his body thrown off Carra rock.

After Krok came Miss Spinks, gliding through the closed window and dripping wet as usual, for she suffered from the Water Madness and was always throwing herself into the well or the duck pond or the moat. She had long hair and was dressed in gray like a Victorian governess (which was what she had been when she was alive), but from being so often in the water her feet had become webbed.

Her story was a sad one. When she was living at Carra, she had fallen hopelessly in love with Rory MacBuff, whose children she had come to teach, and one night, overcome by passion, she had chased him down the corridor with outstretched arms. He had jumped out of the window to get away from her and been killed. After this, Miss Spinks drowned herself in the well, and since ghosts often go on doing what they did when they died, she was almost never dry.

The ghastly creaking of some infernal machine could now be heard. *Squeak . . . creak . . . squeak . . . creak . . .* and through the wall there came a wheelchair and sitting in it an old, old man.

This ancient ghost had been born in distant Transylvania, the son of a poor woman who sent him to the local castle to learn to be a cook. Little Stanislaus soon learned to bake and roast and boil—and he learned, too, to be a vampire. Everyone there sucked blood at night: it was the thing to do, just as in other places it is done to smoke cigarettes. (Actually it is far healthier to be a vampire than a smoker, because blood is full of iron, which is good for you, whereas cigarettes are full of nicotine and tar, which aren't.)

Stanislaus had risen to be head cook when the ninth MacBuff, who was doing a grand tour of Europe, came to visit the castle, bringing his niece, Henny. Henny MacBuff was forty years old at the time, with piggy eyes and a behind so large that she walked through doors sideways. No one thought she would ever find a husband, but she took one look at Stanislaus's black mustache and pale, pointed ears and insisted on marrying him and taking him back to Scotland.

At Carra, Stanislaus (whom they named "Louse," of course) gave up being a vampire. His teeth were giving up in any case, and he settled down to be a good husband to Henny, who was as kind as she was ugly. But after Henny died, life became difficult for him. The new mistress of Carra was a hard woman, and as he grew older and feebler, Uncle Louse was just shoved into corners and forgotten. Then, when he was ninety-nine years old and couldn't see too well, he ran over his own false teeth, crunching them to smithereens under the wheels of his chair. They had been a present from Henny before she died, and after that the old man just lost the will to live. One day he simply drove his wheelchair over the cliff and became a ghost.

There were two more phantoms to come, and Alex waited patiently, for he wanted to speak to all the ghosts at once.

Little Flossie could be heard before she came. A suit of armor crashed to the ground, and then there was the thump of overturning stools, for Carra's youngest ghost was a poltergeist.

Flossie was born at the time when Good Queen Anne was on the throne, and she'd been a pretty child with blond curls, a snub nose, and masses of freckles. But Flossie was born angry. Almost everything annoyed her. She hated porridge and roast beef and milk, and in particular she hated *people*. She bit her nursemaid in the stomach whenever she sang nursery rhymes, and she locked her baby brother in the closet because he looked silly.

Her parents were very much upset by all this, and when Flossie was five years old, they took her to a priest, who said she was possessed by a devil.

"You should put her facedown on the floor," he said, "and jump on her back until the devil comes out of her mouth."

However, before her parents could do this awful thing, Flossie got whooping cough and died.

The last of Carra's ghosts was a dog.

Some dogs can be heard coming by their excited barks or their tails thumping against a door. But when Cyril came, it was the sound of his stomach brushing softly along the rough stone floors that one heard: a gentle sound like the wind in the summer trees or a wavelet leaving a sandy shore.

He was a black dog with a large, whiskery, square-muzzled head; big saucer eyes that were red but full of soul; long eyelashes; and a forked and fiery tongue. So far so good: all hellhounds look like that. But between his head and his tail there was a long, long body—you could have put four dachshunds end to end between the front of Cyril and the back. To carry such a body properly one would need at least eight legs, but Cyril had only four, and short ones at that, so that it was not surprising that his backbone drooped, and his sagging stomach wandered along the ground like a hairy vacuum cleaner. The "phantom drainpipe," the butler called him, which was a good description, but unkind.

Hundreds of years ago, Cyril had had a different name and been a proper hellhound, helping Cerberus, the famous three-headed dog, to guard the gates of the Underworld. Cyril had snapped and growled with the best of them, but he just wasn't built for that kind of work. So the chief devil sent him out into the world above to be a phantom dog and run with the Wild Hunt, that dreaded band of demon hounds that race through the sky, bringing doom and destruction to all who see them.

But the Wild Hunt went very fast, and one day Alex's great-great-great-grandmother (who was then young and beautiful) found the dog whimpering outside the portcullis, licking his poor, sore legs and obviously unable to go any farther.

So she had taken him in and given him the name she would have given to her new baby if it had been a boy (but it wasn't), and Cyril had haunted Carra ever since.

They were all here now. Time to begin.

"Ghosts of Carra," said Alex, clearing his throat, "I bring you grave news."

They came closer. Uncle Louse jammed his ear trumpet into his whiskery ear. Miss Spinks stopped dabbing at one webbed foot with the hem of her skirt and lifted her pale, sad face attentively. Krok Fullbelly put down his sword.

Alex had prepared a speech, but now he found he couldn't go on. A lump came into his throat and he had to shut his eyes to keep in the sudden tears.

Some children are brought up by their parents, some are sent away to boarding school so that it is their teachers who help them to grow up. But Alex had been brought up largely by his ghosts.

Being a baby can be horribly boring. Lying in a pram waiting for someone to come and change your nappy; being plunked into a high chair while some ham-fisted person spoons pulp into your mouth . . . But Alex had never been bored. Skeletal fingers had rocked his cradle; ghostly wheelchairs had galloped over his pram. Miss Spinks had dripped past him, festooning his pillow with duckweed, and when he was shut like a prisoner in his playpen, Flossie had come and hurled his toys around his nursery until he fell over from laughing. Krok Fullbelly had been like a father to the orphaned boy. As for

dogs—Alex had never wanted another dog, not after Cyril.

And it was these ghosts that he was going to send away! *No,* thought Alex wretchedly, *I can't . . . it's impossible.*

But he had given his word to Mr. Hopgood. He had promised—and with a great effort he said, "The castle has been sold. To a gentleman from America."

The ghosts digested this. None of them had been to America, but from haunting the library and the butler's television set, they thought they knew about it, and there was talk of cowboys and Indians and gangsters and Chicago.

"But you won't go away?" asked Krok. Like so many large, strong people, he was very tenderhearted.

"I'll be staying nearby," Alex said. "The headmaster at Errenrigg has offered me a room in his house during the term. But the thing is . . . Mr. Hopgood has a little daughter. She was ill with polio and she's delicate and he won't take any risks with her."

"What sort of risks?" asked Miss Spinks.

"Well, being frightened. By seeing ghosts, for example. Like you."

At first the thought that they were frightening pleased the ghosts. Krok put on his helmet and tipped it over one eye, and Uncle Louse gave a gleeful chuckle. But then, one by one, they became worried.

"You mean we would have to be invisible all the time?" asked Krok.

Alex shook his head. "That wouldn't do, I'm afraid. You couldn't expect Cyril to understand—and Flossie's very young. No, it's worse than that. I'm afraid I . . . I have to ask you to go and live somewhere else."

The silence that fell now was a terrible one. Then Miss Spinks gave a moan and covered her face, and Uncle Louse took out his ear trumpet and poked at it with shaking fingers, not able to believe he had heard what he had heard.

"Somewhere else?" repeated Krok in his deep Viking voice. "How can we go somewhere else? This is our home!"

"It's my home, too," said Alex. "But I'm going. I have to. Carra's got to be looked after properly, and if someone else can do it, we have to help them."

"Then we'll come with you," declared Krok, and little Flossie nodded and sent a couple of mousetraps scudding across the floor.

"I wish you could. But the headmaster's house really wouldn't do. It's just a small semidetached; you'd be miserable there. But I know where you *can* go and where I can come and see you quite often because my mother's cousin still lives there."

"Where's that?"

"Dunloon," said Alex. "Dunloon Hall, down in Northumberland."

The ghosts stared at him, and Cyril, who sensed that all was not as it should be, lifted his head from Alex's feet and howled.

"That trumpery chocolate-box place?" Uncle Louse was so upset that he drove his wheelchair right through Alex. "Why, it's not even five hundred years old!"

"And it's over the border! It's in *England*!" said Krok. Being a Viking, he wasn't actually Scottish at all, but he often *felt* Scottish.

"Ghosts of Carra!" said Alex, making a last desperate effort because he was at the end of his tether. "This is a chance to do something nobler than you have ever done before. Who knows but if you do it, you may be released from the eternal torment of haunting and be summoned back to your home in the skies. Or something. My aunt Geraldine is getting old. Her chest wheezes. She wants to go and live in a hotel. The butler wants to join his brother. The housemaid—"

Krok put up a hairy hand like a police officer.

"Please understand, O Laird of Carra," he rumbled,

"that no one here gives a fig—or a button or a toenail—for the butler. Or the housemaid."

"Or your aunt Geraldine," put in Miss Spinks. "All that fuss just because I made a puddle on the pillow."

"For none of these people would we dream of stirring from our beloved home," Krok went on, looking longingly at the cobwebs, the bat droppings, the pile of rusty thumbscrews on the floor. "In fact we could see them all roasted slowly on a spit and not lose a minute's haunting. No, if . . . *if* we agreed to go somewhere else we would be doing it only for—"

He paused and Alex could see a flush spreading through his ectoplasm, turning his beard to the rich red it had been when he was alive.

"For what?" he asked.

"For you," said Krok Fullbelly.

And then he vanished and, one by one, the ghosts of Carra followed suit.

DUNLOON WAS QUITE different from Carra Castle. It was extremely grand, almost a palace, with statues of gods and goddesses on the terrace and a deer park—and it was a long way from the sea.

Inside, there were salons crammed with satin chairs, and clocks with marble people lying on top of them, and glass cases holding things that were valuable but useless, like snuffboxes or the bed sock that Charles the First had worn before they chopped off his head.

Dunloon belonged to Sir Ian Trottle, a man so stuck-up and snooty that he once spent a whole day sitting on the lavatory because he was too proud to shout for loo paper. It was his wife, Lady Trottle, who was the cousin of Alex's mother. She was silly but good-natured and had always remembered Alex's birthday and sent a present at Christmas.

What Alex hadn't known (because he hadn't stayed there since he was very small) was what a snobbish lot the Dunloon ghosts were.

There is a kind of spook that glides about in a silken crinoline and high heels (if it's a woman) or velvet pants and a powdered wig (if it's a man). Overdressed phantoms like these are not usually up to much except laying a clammy hand on someone's pillow or giving a genteel moan behind the paneling—and it is feeble nonsense like this that gives haunting a bad name.

The Dunloon ghosts were like that. There was the Green Lady, who carried a jeweled fan and spent hours arranging beauty spots on her ectoplasm, and her sister, who was the Red Lady and haunted in a hat decorated with ostrich feathers. And there was a male ghost called Handsome Hal who wasn't handsome at all, but a silly fop whose idea of frightening people was to leave an artistic bloodstain beside their bed.

Alex had telephoned Lady Trottle and explained about his ghosts. She had said, "Of course you can send them, dear," and had even remembered to leave a message in stinkhorn juice on the floorboards of the Long Gallery. But were the Dunloon ghosts pleased that they were going to have visitors? They were not!

"It's abominable, having that uncouth set of spooks

foisted on us," drawled Handsome Hal, fiddling with his cravat.

"That awful old man," said the Green Lady, setting up a nasty draft with her fan. "I mean, a vampire is one thing, but a *cook*!"

"We must think of it as a *duty*," said the Red Lady, who was older than the others and liked to tell them what to do. "After all, poor Lady Trottle's mother had to have evacuees during the war. Dreadful children with lice and cockney accents. Only in the servants' hall, of course."

"I say, that's an idea," said Hal, looking more cheerful. "We could keep them in the servants' hall. Not let them haunt above stairs at all?"

"We shall have to see," said the Red Lady. "Just as long as they don't bring any animals. Animals in the house I cannot *abide*!"

The Carra ghosts left their home on a misty night at the end of June.

Never had the castle looked more beautiful. The seabird droppings glistened white against the slimy stones; ravens cawed on the battlements. Everyone was there to see them go: the rat that lived behind the oak chest in the East Tower, a pair of bats, mother and son, who had stayed behind when the others went to feed. Rows of cockroaches were lined up to say good-bye; the spiders swayed from their threads in sympathy, and a wet friend of Miss Spinks—a river spirit—had come out of the water and sat crying and dripping on a stool.

As always before a journey, there were many things to decide. Should Uncle Louse travel with his head off, which was safer, or with his head on, which would look better when he arrived at Dunloon? Should Cyril be made to wear a collar, which he hated; did Krok need his ax *and* his sword?

Alex was everywhere, lending a hand and giving comfort. It was he who helped Miss Spinks tie up her feet in flannel because she was shy about them being webbed, and it was he who found Flossie's thighbone, which had rolled behind the coal scuttle. (Most young children have something they have to hold before they can go to sleep; a teddy bear, perhaps, or a woolly blanket. With Flossie it was the thighbone of a dead sheep covered in dark green mold, and nothing else would do.)

But at last the parting could be put off no longer. It was a moment so awful that no one could believe it was really happening. Ghosts that are needed and loved are not just transparent splotches that pass through doors and shriek and clank. Their ectoplasm grows firm and strong; they can eat, and they can think and feel as deeply as people who are real.

Since Alex was left an orphan, the ghosts of Carra had shared his life, and they did not see how they could bear to go away.

Again it was Alex who knew what to do. With steady steps he climbed the stairs to the battlements, and in a firm, clear voice he said: "Farewell, ye ghosts of Carra, and may the Spirits of Doom and Darkness go with you on your way."

Then he stood at attention and saluted. The ghosts, seeing how brave he was (though deathly pale), became brave also, and one by one they glided away over the ramparts and turned toward the south.

Everything would have been all right if it hadn't been for Cyril. Cyril, though a hellhound, was only a dog, and had not understood exactly what was going on. He thought they were just going for a little evening glide, for how could anyone expect him to leave Alex? And after bounding through the sky for a mile, the hellhound turned around and raced back, his little legs going like pistons, to land with a thump on Alex's feet and lick him with his fiery tongue and make him see that all was well.

So it all had to be done again—saying good-bye—and this time Alex could not manage to be brave. Long after Cyril's lead had been hitched to the wheelchair and his howls had died away, Alex just sat there as still as stone—and even the ravens and the screech owls respected his sorrow and let him be.

The next day the servants left, and the day after that Alex took his aunt Geraldine to a hotel in Torquay.

Carra was now empty, and on the first day of July, just as he had said he would, Mr. Hopgood came.

Dunloon had no less than one hundred rooms, so it should have been easy enough for the Dunloon ghosts to leave their visitors in peace.

But they didn't. All day long, the Red Lady and the Green Lady, glaring like angry traffic lights, picked on the newcomers and nagged while the namby-pamby Hal with his snuff and his ruffles sneered and drawled.

They didn't like Krok's table manners. He belched, they said, and he ate with his hands, and this was perfectly true. A Viking who drank genteelly from a cup with his little finger crooked around the handle wouldn't have lasted very long, and not only the Northmen but the Chinese think belching is a polite way of showing that you have enjoyed your food.

"And those disgusting beetles in your beard," said the Red Lady. "Really, you might at least comb them out."

But Krok had always had beetles in his beard. They had been there so long that they had passed on and become little phantoms, and Krok wouldn't have dreamed of disturbing them. The braver a man is—and Krok had been very brave—the less he will bully little creatures who cannot defend themselves.

Uncle Louse, of course, was fair game for the toffee-nosed Ladies. They jeered because he mumbled without his teeth and spoke in a Transylvanian accent; they hooted with laughter when he got muddled and put his pipe into his ear and tried to smoke his ear trumpet.

"The old fool ought to be kept out of sight of decent people," said the Green Lady, making sure that Uncle Louse would hear and be hurt by her words—and as early as four o'clock in the afternoon they wanted to know if it wasn't Flossie's bedtime.

Miss Spinks felt their unkindness particularly. She had never got over the fact that Rory MacBuff had jumped out of the window rather than hold her in his arms, and when people were unfriendly, her Water Madness got much worse. One day she got into the bath that a housemaid had been running for Sir Ian Trottle in his private bathroom. When the maid came back to turn off the water and found a gray governess with long hair sitting in the tub, she screamed the place down.

"What on earth are you doing, you ridiculous spook," screeched the Red Lady, swooping in to interfere as usual.

"I'm trying to drown myself," said Miss Spinks miserably. "I always try to drown myself."

"She has the Water Madness," explained Krok, helping her out of the bath.

"Because of my crime," said Miss Spinks, dripping helplessly on to the floor.

But the Ladies didn't want to know about the Water Madness or the guilt Miss Spinks felt about having sent Rory MacBuff to his death. They didn't want to hear about the moment when Uncle Louse's teeth had crunched sickeningly beneath the wheels of his chair. They didn't even want to hear about the curse that had been laid on Krok Fullbelly—though it was an interesting curse and important.

"You will want to know about my curse," Krok had said the first night at dinner—and he had gone on to explain that Viking heroes when they die go to a special heaven called Valhalla, where they eat hog meat and drink barley wine and tell each other stories. But when he, Krok, had been thrown off Carra Rock because he wouldn't go on pillaging and burning and dragging women about by the hair, the priests had cursed him for being a coward. They said he was doomed to go on roaming the earth as an unquiet spirit until he had caused someone's death.

"It's to do with honor," Krok had explained to the

Ladies. "I have to spill blood and then I can stop being a ghost and become a hero. Though I shall still be dead, of course. . . ."

Alex had liked nothing better than to hear about Krok's curse, and they had often discussed how Krok might kill someone and so get up to Valhalla and eat hogs. But the ghosts of Dunloon just yawned and said, "Oh, yes?" They were lousy listeners, though they droned on often enough about what had happened to them. The Red Lady had smothered her husband with a pillow because he snored; the Green Lady had got shut in a closet when deciding which of her ninety-seven dresses to wear and been suffocated; and Hal had fallen into a ditch when drunk—as though anybody cared.

But worst of all was the way the Dunloon ghosts treated Cyril.

"Is he house-trained?" was the first thing the Ladies had asked when the poor dog, half dead with exhaustion, had touched down on their roof. Hal, whenever the hellhound passed him, would wrinkle up his nose and start brushing imaginary hairs off his velvet pants. Cyril knew, of course, and he became, as dogs do when they are not loved, rather puppylike. Before he could get too downhearted, however, someone left the top off a glass case in the Gold Salon and Cyril found the bed sock that had belonged to Charles the First.

Cyril became very fond of this bed sock. Probably it still smelled a little of the sad king's feet. He took it everywhere. But of course when people came, Cyril vanished and the bed sock didn't—and the maids, seeing a free-floating sock about a foot above the ground, screamed even more.

"Do you realize this is a *royal bed sock*!" said the Red Lady furiously. "And look at it now!"

So Cyril's treasure was taken from him, and as the days passed he became sadder and sadder. His stomach sagged ever more until a bald patch developed in its middle from rubbing so hard against the ground.

"We must be brave," said Krok. "We must put up with it for Alex."

Miss Spinks nodded her wet head. "It can't be easy for him, either."

Miss Spinks was right. It was not easy for Alex. He had taken his aunt Geraldine to Torquay and settled her into the Queen's Hotel, which she liked very much. There was a Palm Court orchestra that played waltzes at teatime; delicious cream cakes arrived on trolleys; and the lounges were full of friendly ladies knitting and playing cards. Her room faced the sea; she had her own bathroom with a rose pink bath and a matching washbasin; and the television set was the kind you could turn on and off from the bed.

All the same, when it came to saying good-bye to Alex, Aunt Geraldine, who, after all, had lived with him since he was six months old, became rather weepy, and Alex, instead of going back north, decided to stay with her for a while. There were several weeks to go before the autumn term and, to tell the truth, he was glad to be away from Carra. He knew he'd done the right thing — selling it to Mr. Hopgood, and he hoped that he and Helen would be very happy there, but it is not easy to think of strangers living in your home.

Torquay was very pretty, but the things that pleased Aunt Geraldine were not of very much use to Alex, who didn't really like cream cakes or Viennese waltzes or rose pink bathroom suites. Everyone in the hotel seemed to be old, and Alex missed the clean, cold air of the North and his room in the West Tower.

But most of all, Alex missed his ghosts. He had known it would be difficult to live without them, but it was far worse than he had imagined.

When you are thinking of people, you seem to see them everywhere. Alex would pass an aged person being wheeled along in a Bath chair and turn around with a thudding heart, only to find himself staring into the baleful eyes of some old man with a perfectly good set of teeth. A little girl eating ice cream would make him duck as he waited for her to send a whole pile of cones flying across the beach, but the insipid child just stood there. Again and again, he found himself saying, "I'll ask Krok about that"—and then remember that the Viking was hundreds of miles away. As for the "phantom drain-pipe," Alex could scarcely bring himself to pat the ordinary, solid dogs that romped on the sands, he missed him so much.

Still, he was determined to make the best of things. He made friends with the son of the headwaiter, and together they went to the bowling alley and the skating rink and fished off the pier. Then, a week before he was due back at school, a letter came, forwarded by the headmaster from Errenrig. It was from Mr. Hopgood, and when Alex read it his jaw quite literally dropped open. He read it once more, and then a third time, to see if it really said what he thought it said, and then he went to find Aunt Geraldine.

The following day he was on the train, bound once more for Scotland.

TIME DRAGGED FOR the ghosts at Dunloon. Every day there was a new snub, a new piece of unpleasantness. Sometimes it was a complaint about the duckweed Miss Spinks brought in; once there was a fight because Flossie had got annoyed with a footman and bitten him in the leg—as though any little girl, let alone a poltergeist, could stand the sight of a grown man in satin pants passing around veal chops in a pair of gloves!

It seemed as though the visitors could do nothing right. After the trouble over Sir Ian Trottle's bath, Miss Spinks took to drowning herself in the fountain on the terrace, but the water was so shallow that she could only do it by standing on her head. And here, too, there was a fuss, because Dunloon was open to the public and a lady from Huddersfield in a Crimplene trouser suit, seeing these webbed feet sticking in the air, and a pair of upside-down ghostly gray knickers, fainted clean away.

"It's being unwanted everywhere," said Uncle Louse. "That is what hurts. Unwanted here, unwanted at home."

They were quite ill with homesickness, the poor Carra ghosts, and after dinner when the Ladies and Hal had gone off to tweak at their hair and dab ointments into their ectoplasm, they played the "Do you remember?" game.

"Do you remember those picnics down in the dungeons?" Krok would ask. "That intelligent rat that shared with us. . . . What a natural life we led. How healthy!"

"And the sea!" said Miss Spinks, whose Water Madness was getting worse and worse. "I do so miss the sea."

But they had promised Alex to stay at Dunloon and so they would. What changed their lives was something rather odd: a dead ferret.

The ferret had died of old age and lay in an open drain beside the kitchen garden. There Cyril found it.

Cyril had not sulked when they took away his bed sock, but he had suffered. The ferret, however, cheered him up at once. He really liked it; he thought it might be his younger brother or perhaps his puppy, and he picked it up in his mouth and carried it everywhere. Sometimes he shook it a little and sometimes, when it got a bit limp and squashed-looking, he put it down and licked it into shape, but always and in every way the ferret was his friend.

One day, however, he carried it into the drawing room and put it to bed on the sofa, and Sir Ian Trottle came and sat on it in his best trousers just before he was going out to dinner with the duke of Mortimer, a man so important that he often had the queen to stay.

This time the Ladies were quite beside themselves with fury.

"Do you realize it might have been the *duke himself* who sat on a dead ferret?" screeched the Green Lady.

The ghosts of Carra didn't see that it made any difference *who* sat on a ferret—a duke or a plumber or a dustman; they were not snobbish in the least. But the Red Lady now pointed to Cyril with a shaking hand and said, "Out! Out of this house, you filthy animal, and don't ever set foot in it again! From now on you'll sleep in the cowshed. Even a kennel's too good for you."

"Yes, out to the cowshed!" screamed the Green Lady, and Hal kicked out at Cyril with his buckled shoe.

It is possible that Cyril had never been more hurt than he was at that moment. Even being cast out of hell had not upset him more. Had he been angry, he might have savaged Hal and the Ladies and burned them with his fiery tongue, but what he felt was deeper than anger. And

that night the dog that had helped Cerberus to guard the gates of hell and raced through the star-spangled sky with the Wild Hunt lay in the straw among cows.

Cows are, of course, very useful animals. But to Cyril these large, dozy beasts, standing in rows while bags of milk hung from their underneaths, were a horrid sight. The way they let people pull at their udders, their silly eyes, and all that mooing. . . .

For one hour, and two, and three, Cyril lay with his head between his paws, enduring his shame. Then he got up, shook himself, and padded slowly out into the yard. The night was clear, the moon rising. Carefully, Cyril sniffed the wind. Then he threw back his head and howled—a sound so mournful that it sent the night creatures scuttling away in alarm.

There was only one thing left to do—and Cyril did it.

It was Flossie who found out that the hellhound was missing, and she woke Krok by sitting on his chest and pounding him with her fists.

"Cyril's gone," said the poltergeist. "And Flossie wants him. She wants him *now*."

Krok yawned and scratched his beard. "He's in the cowshed. In banishment."

"No, he's *not*." Flossie's lip began to tremble. "He isn't not *anywhere*."

So Krok woke the others and they all went to look. Flossie was right; there was no sign of the hellhound, but on the soft mud of the farmyard there were unmistakable tracks that pointed to the north, then stopped abruptly where the dog had become airborne.

They all understood then. Cyril had fled to the place where he had been happy. He had gone home.

"Oh, what shall we do?" cried Miss Spinks. "Alex will never forgive us if anything happens to the poor dear creature."

"And yet we promised to stay away from Carra; we gave our word." The Viking was very troubled, for nothing is more binding than a Viking oath.

"There's a chance we might overtake him," said Uncle Louse. "The tracks look fairly fresh. If we can bring him back, there's no harm done."

Ten minutes later, having stopped only to collect a few of their things, the ghosts were in the sky, calling and searching, searching and calling.

It was no use. No drainpipe-shaped creature was hidden among the flocks of traveling geese; no barks came from behind the fleecy clouds . . . and by evening they had reached the estuary that ran inland from Carra Point.

Perhaps it was wrong, but the ghosts now forgot their promise to Alex; they forgot that Helen Hopgood might see them and be frightened—they forgot everything except that at any moment they would once more see beloved Carra with its slime-covered towers, its crazy battlements, the flagpole like a black pencil against the sky!

"Let's close our eyes," said Miss Spinks, beating her webbed feet together girlishly. "Then when I say 'Now' we can open them, and then there it will be!"

"*I* will say 'Now,'" said Krok Fullbelly, taking charge.

So they closed their eyes and glided the last few miles across the estuary.

"Now!" commanded Krok.

The ghosts opened their eyes. Then a great, full-bellied cry of horror came from the Viking; Flossie tumbled from Uncle Louse's lap—and all of them stopped dead in midair.

The castle had gone. Quite simply vanished. The wave-lashed towers were gone. The barbican and the drawbridge and the gatehouse were gone.

Where Carra had stood, proud against the northern sky, there was now only gaping emptiness.

The ghosts never knew how long they hung there, rooted to the sky. Miss Spinks's ectoplasm turned a sickening green, and if Krok hadn't caught hold of her hair, she would have drifted downward in a faint.

"Oh, ruin! Oh, darkness and betrayal! Oh, disaster and despair!" Uncle Louse's ear trumpet trembled in his hand, and little Flossie whimpered and reached for her bone.

"Is it a curse?" wondered Krok. "Have Thor and Odin come to smite our home?"

"Or a storm?" suggested the vampire.

Still supporting the swaying governess, they floated slowly to the ground. No storm could have done what had been done to Carra, and if it was a curse, it was a very strange one. Every stick and stone of what had once been Carra had vanished, but the bare ground was clear of rubble and the foundations stood out plainly: the underground passages, the place where the well had been.

"The nasty man's stolen the castle," said Flossie. "Flossie's going to bite him in the stomach; Flossie's going to kick him in—"

"Hush," said Krok. "It's his castle now. There can be no talk of stealing."

But if it was Mr. Hopgood's doing, why had he done it? Why had he destroyed something for which he had paid so much?

It was then that they heard high, excited barking coming from the landward side of the castle. Cyril, at least, was found! The ghosts glided quickly across the moat— and saw a most extraordinary sight!

Parked on the narrow roadway that led to Errenrig was a fleet of trucks—about twenty of them—standing nose to tail facing away from Carra. The trucks were open and each one was piled high with stones of all kinds: round ones, square ones, carved ones—and on each stone was a squiggly mark in yellow paint.

"It's the castle! It's the castle on the trucks!" squeaked the poltergeist excitedly.

"The child speaks truly," said Krok. "Look, there are the pillars from the banqueting hall; I know them well."

"And that slab with the poor dear snail in it," said Miss Spinks, pointing with a shaking finger. "That's from the armory."

Another volley of barks led them to the first of the trucks, where the hellhound was crouched, digging with his little forefeet as though his life depended on it. Though he was overjoyed to see them, Cyril only had time to clout them a few times with his wagging tail before he turned back to his explorations. And no wonder! For this truck didn't just contain stones. It was full of things they knew well: the old chest, the suit of armor, the rusty thumbscrews. . . . It was their own East Tower that was piled up here.

"Oh, what can it all mean?" wailed Miss Spinks. "It's all so *strange!*" And suddenly her knees gave way and she collapsed on a carved door, her webbed feet pointing at the sky.

"We must rest," said Krok Fullbelly firmly. "What it

means will be shown in the devil's own time, but now we can do no more."

Even he, who could lift an ox when he was alive, was tired, and Uncle Louse was quite blue with shock and strain. So they made themselves as comfortable as they could on the truck. Flossie curled up beside Cyril, and one by one they closed their eyes.

Ghosts who have suffered sleep like the dead. So slept the ghosts of Carra now, becoming invisible as spirits do in slumber—nor did they wake when the men came in the morning and drove the trucks across the country to Liverpool, where the world's biggest ship, the *Queen Anne,* lay waiting at anchor, ready for her journey across the sea.

MR. HOPGOOD WAS not insane, nor was he a thief. He was just a man who liked Scottish castles but did not like the Scottish winter. Also, he couldn't spend a lot of time in Scotland because he needed to look after his oil wells and his factories and his department stores.

So he decided to buy a Scottish castle, have it pulled down very carefully, and rebuild it in America where he lived.

He had not told his daughter, Helen, what he was going to do because he wanted it to be a surprise. And he didn't tell Alex beforehand because he thought it might be rather a shock for the boy. But when the workmen had finished at Carra, he wrote Alex a letter, and this is what it said:

Dear Alex,

As you may have heard by now, I have finished pulling down Carra Castle and am arranging to have it shipped back to the States on the *Queen Anne,* sailing from Liverpool on September 3.

It's been on my mind to ask if you'd like to come and watch over the rebuilding of the castle in my hometown of Granite Falls in Texas?

I've found a really nice spot for it not too far from my present home, and I reckon you could be most useful in making sure that everything is put back exactly as it was. I plan to have the job finished in a couple of months, and then I'm going to give a Scottish ball to celebrate. If you could stay over for that, it would be an honor: to have a proper MacBuff present at such an occasion would give the best possible send-off to the place.

Of course, I'd expect you to be my guest during the rebuilding, and I'll pay your fare across the Atlantic because I know you've put the money I paid you in trust for when you're grown up. There's a direct plane from Heathrow to Houston, and you'd be collected there and driven to my place.

I'm off back home next week, so let my secretary in London know what you prefer. I'm sure that you and Helen will get along splendidly.

With best wishes,
Yours sincerely,
Hiram C. Hopgood

This was the letter Alex had been reading in Torquay.
Now he stood in the headmaster's study at Errenrig,
waiting to hear if Mr. Donaldson would let him miss the
autumn term at school.

It was a difficult decision for a head teacher to make.
School is school and lessons are important. The head
had read Mr. Hopgood's letter and now stood looking
out of the window and thinking hard.

"It's a chance, Alex—a real chance," he said at last.
"I've never been to America myself, let alone Texas. The
Lone Star State, they call it. . . . Of course you'd have to
work like a demon when you got back, but you're well
ahead in most of your studies. Yes, if the trustees in
Edinburgh agree, you can go."

The trustees did agree. They had heard of Mr. Hopgood and knew that Alex would be safe with him. So
Alex wrote at once to Mr. Hopgood's secretary, and
she booked him on a plane from Edinburgh to London
and on a jumbo jet from London to Houston. She also
rang the airport staff and asked them to look out for a
twelve-year-old boy who was traveling alone and see
that he was all right.

There was only one more thing for Alex to decide:
should he go to Dunloon before he left and say good-bye
to his ghosts?

He thought about this a lot, but in the end he decided

against it. The headmaster had often told him how unsettled children became when they first went to boarding school and their parents visited too soon. He would go straight away when he got back from America; perhaps they could all spend Christmas together. But the truth was, he himself couldn't face another parting.

And three days after the *Queen Anne* steamed out of harbor, Alex flew out from London, bound for Mr. Hopgood's house in Granite Falls.

"COME ALONG, DEAR, you haven't taken your pills," said the nurse to Helen Hopgood.

She wore a white smock, her voice was brisk and jolly, and she held out a bottle of red pills.

"I've had my pills," said Helen. "I had the green ones after lunch. And I had the blue ones after breakfast."

"But not the red ones!" said Nurse, still jolly, but in a steely way. "You' know your father likes you to have all of them. And then it's time for your rest."

"I'm not tired," said Helen. "Please don't make me rest again."

But there was no getting around Nurse Boniface, who had been engaged to look after Helen since her illness, and who spent her days making Helen take medicine and disinfecting her room and rubbing her legs with an ointment that was supposed to make them strong again, but smelled absolutely vile.

Nurse Boniface was a good nurse, and the doctor who came every week to prod and poke Helen's joints was a good doctor, and the physical therapist who came to massage her was the very best. Mr. Hopgood worried so much about Helen that he had surrounded her with people who were supposed to make her completely well.

Only Helen wasn't getting completely well. If you spend all day eating pills and having people take your temperature and telling you to rest, you just get iller. Helen was small for her age and pale, and though her limp wasn't a bad one, it was still there.

The house that Helen lived in with her father was called Green Meadows. It was long and low like a ranch house and had nine bathrooms, a swimming pool, and a small cinema where Helen could watch films. There were buttons everywhere to press and make the air-conditioning come on, or beautiful music play—and at night the terrace was lit up by hundreds of different-colored lights.

But around the garden of Green Meadows there was a high chain-link fence, and the top of the fence was electrified. A guard with two fierce dogs—Doberman pinschers who bit first and asked questions afterward—

patrolled the grounds. The gates were electronically operated and opened only after you had identified yourself to the man who lived in the lodge.

All this was necessary because Mr. Hopgood was a millionaire and had to stop burglars getting in to steal his pictures or kidnappers getting in to snatch his daughter. But Helen did feel very much like the Sleeping Beauty must have felt when the hedge of thorns grew over her house. "Except that I'm not beautiful," Helen said sadly to herself.

This was true. Helen was too thin; there were often dark circles under her eyes, and her long brown hair seemed too heavy for her head. When Helen smiled, she lit up like a candle and no one cared whether she was beautiful or not, but she did not smile very often. For Helen had come to believe that she would never get well, or be like other children and go to school. And sometimes, lying awake in the dark, she thought that quite soon she was going to die.

But today her rest passed quickly and she did whatever Nurse Boniface asked her to do, for her father was expected back from Great Britain. He had already phoned and told her that he had the most exciting news!

Mr. Hopgood had flown all night across the Atlantic, but as soon as he arrived in Houston, he had himself driven straight to the Hopgood Building in the center of town.

The building had eighty-seven stories and all of them belonged to him. On the first twenty-three were the offices of the people who looked after his oil wells. The next thirty-nine floors housed the people who looked after his department stores, and the rest of the building was for the people who managed his factories.

Mr. Hopgood himself had a suite of rooms on the top floor with a rubber plant and a tank of tropical fish and some black sofas. But he had no time to look at the rubber plants or feed the fish or sit on the sofas, because as soon as he arrived, absolutely everyone wanted to tell him what they had bought and done and sold while he was away.

All day Mr. Hopgood worked at his desk. His secretaries went out to lunch, but Mr. Hopgood stayed and had lunch brought in on a tray. It was not a very nice lunch: a bowl of semolina and a glass of milk. The worries of being a millionaire had made his stomach squirt out so much acid that a sore place had developed—an ulcer—and when he ate anything at all rough or interesting, he got a pain.

But at last the day was over and he left the Hopgood Building and was driven to his home in Granite Falls. Mr. Hopgood had looked dreadfully tired when he left his office, but now he began to relax, and even to smile—for he was driving toward the person he loved most in the world: his daughter, Helen.

It was very late when Mr. Hopgood got in, but Helen was wide-awake, sitting up in her nightdress and waiting.

"Now then," said Mr. Hopgood when they'd finished hugging each other. "Let's see how good you are at guessing. What do you think I bought over in Britain?"

Helen guessed and guessed, but she didn't come anywhere near the truth.

"A castle!" said Mr. Hopgood, beaming. "A real, genuine Scottish castle!"

Helen stared at him and her eyes grew wide. "Are we going to live in Scotland, then?" she asked eagerly, for she had read all about the Battle of Glencoe and Robert the Bruce with his spider and, of course, Bonnie Prince Charlie hiding in caves.

Mr. Hopgood shook his head. "There's no way I could go and live over there, darlin'; my work keeps me here. But I'm having the castle shipped home and we're going to put it up right here in Granite Falls. Then when it's all finished, you and I'll move in and be as happy as cows in clover."

"Perhaps there'll be a ghost?" suggested Helen. "Ghosts can travel with an old building even if the stones are separate. I've read it somewhere."

Mr. Hopgood had read it, too. That was why he had been so firm with Alex.

"No, honey," he said. "Absolutely no ghosts—I made sure of that. There'll be nothing to scare my little girl, I promise."

Then he told Helen all about finding Carra and how he had bought it from the owner, who was an orphan and only twelve years old, and Helen listened with wonder and amazement.

What excited her even more than hearing about the castle was the news that Alex was coming to stay, and long after her father had said good night, she lay in bed, wondering what he would be like. *Very tall,* she thought, *with coal black hair and piercing eyes.* She saw him in his kilt and sporran, with sunburned knees, and perhaps the claw of some animal pinned to his beret. He would be riding a horse, of course, and playing the bagpipes, though not at the same time. It was probably difficult to play the bagpipes on a horse.

How were they going to find a haggis for him to eat? she wondered. She knew what a haggis was: the stomach of a sheep filled with old bits of scrunched-up meat, but however loathsome it sounded, they would have to get one. One had to be polite.

After a while she got out of bed and switched on the light and looked at herself in the mirror. Pale and undersized, a girl with a limp who couldn't do *anything* . . . How dreadfully a boy like that would despise her! Well, there was nothing to be done. Helen went back to bed, but it was a long, long time before she slept.

THE *QUEEN ANNE* left Liverpool on a sunny day in September, bound for New York. She was not only the largest ship in the world, but by far the grandest. There were four huge staterooms with raised platforms on which orchestras could play at night, and two dining rooms as big as railway stations, and shops, and a library, and a gym. The passengers were served five-course meals by smiling waiters in red coats, and there was a whole army of stewards and stewardesses to make people comfortable in their cabins.

But better than all the grand rooms below was the open deck. It was a clear white world up there: the scrubbed boards, the gleaming paint, the trim lifeboats in their davits. Gentlemen in blazers strode up and down breathing in the wonderful air; tired ladies lay in rows in steamer chairs with rugs over their knees, tilting their faces to the sun.

At the end of the second day, however, all this changed because the ship ran into a storm.

It was a bad one—a force-ten gale that made the ship heave and judder and slap herself down sickeningly on the waves. First the deck emptied of people and then the staterooms down below emptied. Greedy men who had sat peering at the menu turned green and groped their way to their cabins; drinks were left untouched at the bar; and a lady who was having her hair done tottered away to her bunk, her rollers still on her head. Soon there wasn't a passenger to be seen—only the crew, keeping the storm-bucketed ship on course.

But down in the hold, the ghosts of Carra woke.

Krok woke first and clutched his belly, which did not feel full of food but of uproar and pain. He had no idea where he was or what had happened, but he felt iller than he had ever felt in his life. Then the front wheels of Uncle Louse's chair appeared, followed by the old man himself, clutching his head and groaning.

"It is the heaving sickness, the dreaded plague! We are as good as dead," cried Krok, forgetting that he was dead already.

A swirling ball of force beside them turned into Flossie, her curls bedraggled, the corners of her mouth turned down. "Flossie wants a bucket!" wailed the poltergeist.

"I must go and drown myself!" Miss Spinks rose from behind a pillar. Her lank hair lay across her face; her teeth chattered. "I must drown myself at *once*!"

They *all* wanted to drown themselves. There is nothing like seasickness for making you want to end your life. It was a thousand years since Krok had sailed in his longboat and the juddering and thumping of the great engines were like nothing he had ever known. The worst hit was poor Cyril, whose stomach was so long that when anything went wrong with it he felt it acutely. He now lay moaning on his side with his eyes closed and his long eyelashes tangled and matted on his cheeks.

Not only did they feel dreadfully ill, but they had no idea where they were. They seemed to be in a kind of vault or tomb, but how had they got there?

"It is Hades! It is the Underworld! I am here because of my curse. It's because I haven't killed anyone!" said Krok.

This annoyed Uncle Louse. "Rubbish! The curse is *your* curse and we're all here. What we need is *air*!"

So they all floated up out of the black tomb (which was actually a large metal container in the hold of the ship) and up . . . up . . . until they reached the deck.

The wind met them then: screaming, tearing, buffeting. They could scarcely stand, but they knew now where they were: on a ship in the middle of the ocean! But how had they got there? And where were they going?

"Wait . . . I remember. . . ." The shock of the storm had begun to clear Krok's head. "We fell asleep on a truck . . . on the stones of the castle. . . . So we must have been loaded onto the ship with them. Only why? . . ."

The ghosts, knowing nothing of Mr. Hopgood's plans, could make no sense of this.

But Miss Spinks wasted no time in remembering. Her eyes glittered with the Madness, and before the others could stop her, she had gathered up her skirts and leaped onto the rails.

"I am coming!" cried Miss Spinks to the Atlantic Ocean—and with an eerie scream, she gave herself to the sea.

It was a bad moment. When Miss Spinks gave herself to the duck pond or the well, they knew she would return—but this heaving, pounding mass of gray went on and on, and when Flossie waved her little hand and said, "Bye-bye, Spinkie," she spoke for them all.

None of them would have believed that they could mind so much. The governess had often annoyed them—her wetness, her sadness—but she had *belonged.* Uncle Louse turned his wheelchair away because he didn't want Krok to see how upset he was, and the Viking stood clinging to the rails and shaking his great head to and fro. Even their seasickness seemed unimportant compared with their new sorrow.

In spite of the storm, the ship was moving at a good fifteen knots, so that what happened next was quite extraordinary.

A long whitish arm . . . a tentacle . . . reared out of the water . . . and another . . . and another. Arms studded with suckers, and so long that the ghosts did not believe what they were seeing. Then two more of the pale, snakelike arms groped upward in an exploring way, reaching almost as high as the rails of the ship.

And still another arm—but this one held something in its coils: a limp and bedraggled object like a large and squidgy dishmop.

For an instant the creature itself appeared above the waves, and they saw its round, jellylike body and bulging blue-tinged eyes. Then it vanished, but the arm that held the dishmop now reared up again and, with incredible strength, threw its burden onto the deck.

Then it, too, vanished and there was only the restless, heaving sea.

The ghosts huddled together, trembling. "It was the Blob!" said Uncle Louse wonderingly. "The Big Blob itself! That I should live to see the day!"

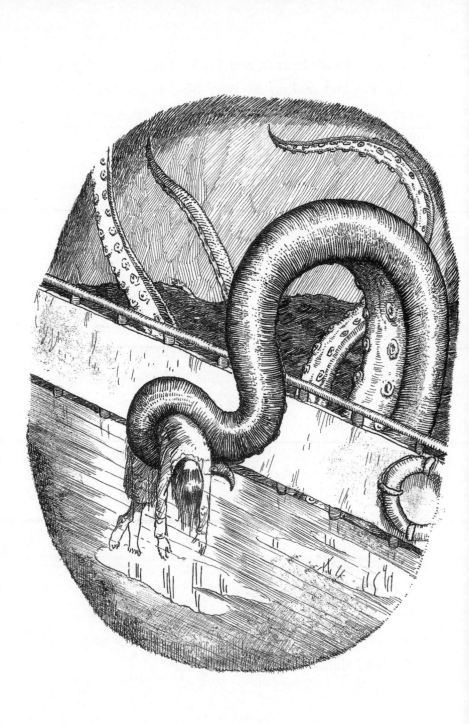

Krok nodded. There was no doubt about it—they had seen the largest sea creature in the world: the giant octopus that men have sought for hundreds of years.

"Why didn't the Blob come and see Flossie?" asked the poltergeist angrily, stamping her feet. It was only people that annoyed her, and she'd liked the octopus very much.

But Cyril, who had been sniffing at the thing that the Blob had hurled onto the deck, had begun to bark excitedly, and they glided over to investigate.

It was not a dishmop. Gray and bedraggled, the governess lay splattered on the deck.

The Viking, who knew about first aid, began at once to chafe her wrists. "Miss Spinks?" he said. "Speak to us, Miss Spinks."

The battered specter moaned. Her eyes fluttered open. "Lettice," she said faintly.

"Lettuce?" Krok had been very upset when she went overboard, but now he was cross again. What did she want a lettuce for? Ghosts *can* eat, but they don't have to—and anyway he hated salad: slithery green stuff with nothing you could get your teeth into.

"It . . . is . . . my Christian name," murmured Miss Spinks, looking deeply into Krok's eyes.

The Viking flushed. He had not realized that Miss Spinks was fond of him. But he was made of sterner stuff than Rory MacBuff. He wasn't going to throw himself out of the window and he certainly wasn't going to call her by a daft name like Lettice.

The ghosts spent the rest of the night in one of the lifeboats slung above the deck. When they woke it was to an entirely different day.

The wind had dropped; the sea was calm; the sun shone. Even as they yawned and stretched, about twenty passengers, many of them fat ladies in very short shorts, came through a door and lined up in rows. Then a young man in a tracksuit came and shouted things at them, and all the people bent down and touched their toes and raised their arms, or lay on the ground bicycling in the air with their pink, plump legs.

It was a fitness class, and Uncle Louse absolutely loved it.

"Oh, if only I had my teeth," he mumbled, for the vampire in him was not entirely dead, and it was years since he had seen such inviting flesh.

Meanwhile, the sailors had uncovered the swimming pool, and a lot more people came running out in rude little bathing costumes that scarcely covered them and leaped into the water, laughing and splashing and throwing colored balls about. Miss Spinks was dreadfully shocked.

"Why do they behave as though drowning oneself was a joke?" she wanted to know.

"Well, you see, they aren't wicked like us," explained Krok. "They haven't committed a crime. They didn't make Rory MacBuff jump out of the window."

There was no doubt about it, the passengers on the *Queen Anne* really enjoyed themselves. The ghosts, gliding about unseen and watching, were quite amazed by shipboard life.

The way people ate in the dining room, for instance. Valhalla—where Krok would have gone to eat hog meat if he hadn't been cursed—was nothing to the dining room of the *Queen Anne*. The waiters served shrimp cocktail followed by grilled sole followed by roast beef and Yorkshire pudding followed by peach melba followed by cheese.

"Why don't the people go 'pop'?" Flossie wanted to know.

But there was no answer to that. They should have gone "pop," but they didn't.

At night there were dances in the ballroom, or music playing in the smaller lounges, and the ghosts liked all of it—except the Zugorsky Trio.

The Zugorskys played slimy sorts of tunes with soppy titles, which they announced in a strong foreign accent, and the ghosts simply could not bear them. It wasn't just the gooey music that they played; it was something creepy and unpleasant about the trio themselves.

Madame Zugorsky was huge and wore a glittering silver dress that made her look like an oversized trout. She had a head full of yellow curls, which were arranged in a sort of tower and fell over her forehead, and she pounded the piano so hard with her great hands that the ghosts feared for the poor keys. On the other hand, her husband, Mr. Zugorsky, was so weedy and pimply and small that when he came onto the platform with his cello, they didn't see how he was ever going to get it between his legs. As for Carmen Zugorsky, Madame Zugorsky's sister, she had long black hair and swayed about with her violin, closing her eyes and *feeling* the music in a most sickening way.

Yet it was from the creepy Zugorskys that the ghosts learned what was to happen to Carra Castle.

Krok had got his sea legs now and often strode around the deck, remembering the days when he had been on a longship and brought terror to the people on the shore.

He was just passing one of the cabins on B deck when he heard voices and saw Madame Zugorsky's blond sausage curls framed in the open porthole.

"Are you sure that's what he's going to do?" Madame

was saying in her deep voice, and Krok stopped, surprised, because she had quite lost her foreign accent. "Build the castle up again in Granite Falls and live there with his kid? In Texas?"

"Of course I'm sure," snapped Carmen Zugorsky, tossing back her long black hair. "I don't make mistakes. The foreman who's in charge of the stuff down in the hold knew all about it."

Krok moved forward, desperately excited.

"If we wait until he's got it built up, it should be a breeze." It was still Carmen talking, and she, too, had dropped her foreign accent. "The place he's in now is worse than Fort Knox to get into."

"But we can't wait that long," squeaked weedy Mr. Zugorsky. "It'll take ages to build up a bloomin' castle."

"We can wait exactly as long as it takes to do a proper job," said Carmen silkily. She hadn't raised her voice, but the little man backed away and banged his behind on his cello case.

"EEEKH! AAGH!" The sudden screams came from Madame Zugorsky. She was clutching her huge bosom with one hand; the other pointed at the deck. "A b-beard . . . hanging in the air . . . a bed reared . . . I mean a red beard!" Her teeth were chattering, and she was the color of cottage cheese.

Krok turned around to see what she had seen, but

there was nobody behind him. Then he realized that he had been careless. A ghost that wants to stay invisible needs to keep his mind on what he's doing and he had been too excited by what he had heard to pay attention. Quickly, he vanished. At the same time the porthole was slammed shut. But Krok had heard enough. Carra was to be rebuilt, its proud towers reaching for the sky! Even if they themselves could no longer haunt the castle, they would be able to watch over their old home. And surely, somehow, they would find a way of getting a message back to Alex in Scotland. Mr. Hopgood would be certain to keep in touch with the boy. Once Alex knew what was happening to them, he would know what to do. Alex knew everything!

Happier than he had been since they'd left Carra, Krok went off to find the others and give them the good news.

8

HELEN HAD BEEN waiting all afternoon for the sound of her father's car. He had gone to the airport to fetch Alex and she was getting more and more nervous. Not about herself—there was nothing to be done about *her.* Alex, with his piercing eyes and his sunburned knees, wasn't going to waste two minutes on her, she knew that, but she had thought he might like the haggis.

Helen had told the cook what a haggis was, and though Maria hadn't really believed her, she had gone to the butcher and told *him.* In fact, quite a lot of people in Granite Falls had had good ideas about what went into a haggis. The garage attendant said that bits of windpipe were important, and the ironmonger (whose grandmother came from Skye) said he remembered her mentioning minced arteries—those thick white ones that took blood from the heart.

Maria had worked hard all day, chopping and stuffing and steaming, but it was difficult for Helen to believe that anything ought to make the kind of smell that was coming from the kitchen. Not that it was any good blaming Maria. She came from Puerto Rico and you can't get much farther from Scotland than that.

If Helen was feeling nervous about meeting Alex, Alex wasn't exactly looking forward to meeting Helen. They had stopped off at the Hopgood Building on the way from the airport, and the way everyone bowed and scraped to Mr. Hopgood had made Alex realize just how rich and important he was. The daughter of a man like that would be thoroughly spoiled and used to ordering everyone about. Not that he cared, really—she'd better not try bossing *him* about; but perhaps it was a pity that the baby he'd sat next to on the airplane had done quite so much finger painting with its spinach on his jeans.

Otherwise, though, Alex liked Texas: the warm sun, the wide cars cruising like ships along the freeways, the flowering thorn trees. Granite Falls was a two-hour drive away from Houston in open countryside, and wherever you looked you seemed to be able to see for miles and miles and miles.

But when they drew up outside the gates of Green Meadows, Alex was shocked. Getting out of Wormwood Scrubs couldn't have been more difficult than getting into Mr. Hopgood's home. It was a full five minutes before the dogs stopped barking and the buzzers stopped buzzing and the electronically operated gates lifted to let them through. Being a millionaire, it seemed to Alex, was no joke.

But at last they drove between smooth green lawns watered by sprinklers and trim flower beds, and drew up at the front door. A small girl with long dark hair was waiting at the top of the steps—and when she saw Alex she looked, for some reason, terribly surprised.

Two hours later, they sat at supper in the luxurious dining room with its beautiful paintings and embroidered rugs.

Mr. Hopgood couldn't eat much because of his acid stomach, but the food so far had been delicious. They'd had big, juicy shrimp cooked in a creamy sauce and corn bread with parsley butter—and the second course looked as though it was going to be just as nice. Maria, the cook, who had a gold tooth and a beaming smile, had brought in a dish of tomatoes and peppers and a bowl of fluffy rice.

But the meat that went with this seemed to be odd. On a big plate in the middle of the table lay something that looked like a football that had suddenly come out in awful boils.

Still, Alex wouldn't have dreamed of refusing it. Perhaps it was some special American dish like hominy grits, which he had read about, though no one had been able to tell him what it was. He put a forkful in his mouth and somehow managed to keep it there. A MacBuff of Carra didn't spit things out—not when he was a guest in someone's house.

"Is it all right?" asked Helen anxiously. "Does it taste nice?"

She had been too shy to say much when Alex came, and then he had gone to his room to unpack, so that he hadn't seen much of her yet, but it obviously mattered to her that he liked this truly fiendish meat.

Alex nodded and gulped down what seemed to be a mangled tapeworm mixed with a piece of shredded rubber glove. "Does it have a name?" he asked politely. "I mean, is it a Texan national dish?"

Helen looked at him in amazement. Then suddenly she began to laugh. She laughed so much that it seemed as if she would fall off her chair.

"It's . . . a . . . haggis," she managed to splutter. "At least, we thought it was!"

"Oh!"

Alex's mouth began to twitch; then he, too, began to laugh, and presently it all came out—how Helen had thought he would be six feet tall with piercing eyes, and how he had thought she would shout and order people about and sneer at his jeans.

After that, Helen forgot her shyness, and when supper was over she showed him her books.

"Oh, you've got *Land of the Tempest*," Alex said excitedly. "That's a marvelous book, isn't it? That's where I'm going first of all—to Patagonia. To find the giant sloth. I'm sure it's not extinct!"

"I'm sure, too," said Helen. "Why should it be? After all, when Prichard went in 1902 they'd just found some sloth hairs in a cave. Why *should* it be extinct? Will you go to the West Coast? Where there are hummingbirds and parrots right up to the snow line?"

"Yes, I will." Alex was perfectly confident. "I want to go to the places that Darwin went to in the *Beagle*. The weather's the trouble, but if one has proper equipment it'll be all right."

"You're so lucky!" Helen's head rested on her hand like in the photograph that Alex had seen and her voice was very wistful. "I'd give anything in the world to go to places like that."

"Well, why don't you?" Alex was studying a map in the book, seeing in his mind the forests and the glaciers and the fjords with icebergs like fantastic castles floating on the water.

"How can I?" Helen's voice was very low, and she touched, with a forlorn gesture, her weak leg.

Alex thought she was being stupid and he said so.

"Your leg's bound to get better. Everything gets stronger as you get older, so why not your leg? Anyway, in most of those places you don't *have* to walk; you can go by canoe—or on a mule." Then he said something that he hadn't meant to say, it just came out. "You could come on my expedition if you like, when I've got it ready. If you wanted to."

Helen didn't say anything—not a word—but from that moment on she gave up the idea that she was soon going to die. There were far more interesting things to think about, now, than that!

The following morning, Mr. Hopgood took Alex to see the site on which he was going to build the castle. Alex had expected them to drive to a place far out in the country—perhaps a desert with prickly pears and a view of the hills like in a Western. He'd thought that Carra would look very good in a place like that. But Mr. Hopgood had decided to rebuild the castle in the middle of Granite Falls, where the people could be proud of it, and where there were shops and good roads. A few years earlier, he'd bought a large field between the Rex Cinema and the Skyway Motel, thinking he might build a factory on it. It was this field that he had chosen for Carra, and now he pointed out to Alex all the advantages: the level ground, the good drainage, and a main road handy so that he could get to his office in Houston without delay.

"You see, I reckon life's pretty lonely for Helen out where we are. You have to be so careful about security. But here in town there'll be more company for her."

Alex saw the sense of this. After all, there was no reason why one shouldn't have a castle between a cinema and a hotel, with a garage across the road.

"The *Queen Anne* docks tomorrow," said Mr. Hopgood. "So the trucks should be here within the week— and then we'll engage the workmen and put the skids under them. I've allowed two months for the rebuilding. We'll have the Opening Ball the week before Christmas."

"As soon as that?" Alex was impressed.

Mr. Hopgood nodded. "What I do, I *do*."

O N THE DAY before the *Queen Anne* was due in New York, Flossie saw something that surprised her. Like all small children, she was very curious and she liked nothing better than to float through the cabins as the ladies and gentlemen inside them were cleaning their teeth and preparing to go to bed.

She was just passing through the Zugorskys' cabin on B deck when she stopped and her little mouth dropped open.

Madame Zugorsky was standing in the middle of the floor. She had wriggled out of her silver fish-scale dress, which had fallen to the ground. Now she lifted her petticoat over her head and stood there in her pants and bra. Her legs were the hairiest Flossie had ever seen and her knees were like doorknobs.

It was the next part, though, that was so strange. Madame Zugorsky took off her bra—and her bosom came off with it! Flossie couldn't believe her eyes, but it was so. Madame Zugorsky's bosom now lay on the dressing table—and what was left on her was just a flat place covered with curly hair.

Flossie was so amazed that she glided straight back to Miss Spinks and told her what she had seen, but the governess only told her not to be rude.

"A lot of ladies need a little help in front," said Miss Spinks, sighing, for she herself was very flat-chested. "Padding is not at all unusual."

But Flossie said it wasn't padding, it was *all* of it. No one, however, listened to the little girl, though she was perfectly correct and had made a most important discovery.

The pianist of the Zugorsky trio was, in fact, a man.

The following morning, they came into harbor.

"Now, remember," urged Krok, "we must keep right on top of the stones down in the hold. If we get separated from the castle when they come to unload, we're lost."

But the ghosts couldn't resist gliding up on deck for a quick look at New York's famous skyscrapers and the huge Statue of Liberty with its bronze arm lifted, welcoming the tired people who came from Europe.

"Ah, how beautiful," sighed Miss Spinks, and all around them the American passengers dabbed their eyes and sniffed because they were coming home.

The poltergeist, though, did not care in the least about the view. She stood by the rails, her fierce little eyebrows drawn together in a scowl and her green eyes searching the muddy water.

Flossie was looking for the Blob.

From the moment that the creature had surfaced and stared with its bulging eyes at the ship, Flossie had loved it. All through the voyage she had longed for it to come again so that she could talk to it and touch its sinister suckers and give it things to eat. She'd waited and waited, and now they were leaving the ship and still it hadn't come.

"Blob?" called Flossie in her high, piping voice. "Are you there, Blob?"

"Shh!" The governess looked around anxiously. The ghosts were all invisible, of course, but Flossie's voice carried a long way.

Saying "Shh!" to a poltergeist is a mistake. Flossie's pearly teeth ground together, she tugged her left ear—and the next moment, every single hat on the head of every passenger rose into the air, did a somersault, and flew overboard.

But before the amazed passengers could find out what had happened, the sound of the ship's engines died away and the gangways were lowered.

They had arrived.

The Zugorsky Trio left the *Queen Anne* along with the other passengers and were driven to a hotel room in Manhattan.

There a number of things happened.

First, Madame Zugorsky took off her high-heeled shoes and her pearls and her dress. Then she took off her wig. Lastly, she took off her petticoat and the bra with the two pink balloons that Flossie had seen and put them on the dressing table.

What was left now was a heftily built man in his underpants. He had a cropped head of blond hair, pale blue eyes, and almost colorless eyelashes. His name was Oscar Pickering, but he was also known as the Hulk or the Albino, and he was as brutal and thickheaded a thug as you could imagine.

Since Madame Zugorsky was a man, it follows that weedy little Mr. Zugorsky was not her husband. In fact, Mr. Zugorsky, who was now wriggling out of his tight black shoes, was a petty crook called Ratty Banks who'd begun to steal almost before he could walk.

Meanwhile, Carmen Zugorsky was tugging at her long black hair, which came off suddenly, leaving her with a short, grizzled crop like an old-fashioned schoolmarm's. Then she wiped off her heavy makeup, took out her contact lenses, and put on a pair of spectacles with thin steel rims.

The woman who now stood peering at herself in the mirror looked like a respectable middle-aged spinster, but of the three of them she was by far the most dangerous and the one the police wanted to catch most of all.

"Well, we made it," said Oscar the Hulk, fingering his scar. It was a jagged scar on his forehead, and he told people he'd got it in a fight outside a pub, but actually it had been made by a small girl called Simonetta Briggs who had hit him with a lemonade bottle in the school yard because he kicked her brother's dog.

The woman by the mirror turned. "What do you mean, we've made it?" she snapped. "We've not begun. We have to get to Granite Falls, we have to make contact with the Bulgoni brothers, we have to infiltrate the house. . . ."

"All right, all right. I only said—"

"Well, don't. Don't say anything. I don't want to hear from you," she spat, and the Hulk shut his mouth.

Oscar had had a good start in life. His parents were respectable butchers who sent him to an expensive school and paid for piano lessons and always saw that he was nicely dressed.

The bad streak in Oscar came from inside him. He began by stealing cats and dogs off the street and selling them to be minced up for pet food. By the time he was fifteen, he had stolen a van and was rounding up wild ponies from the New Forest and getting fifty pounds apiece from the knackers for their carcasses. He was eighteen when he killed his first man—a gamekeeper whom he strangled with his bare hands when the man tried to stop him dragging a mare away from her foal.

After that, Oscar was on the run, but the police never caught up with him—perhaps because the picture they put out of him as a wanted man looked so peculiar that no one could believe he was real. And yet it was a good likeness; the Hulk did have a flat nose, fat lips, and eyes like frozen frog eggs.

As for Ratty, he'd been the kind of boy who starts by stealing his schoolmates' pencils and erasers and goes on to steal their bicycles and cars. People had done their best for Ratty—in one reform school they'd even taught him to play the cello—but he was never out of prison for long.

But the mastermind, and the person who really mattered, was the woman.

She'd been christened Janet Batters, and she was one of seven sisters whose mother brought them up to play in a band called The Beautiful Batters. The band was a success, but Janet never fitted in. She was odd from the start. Then one day she found a picture of Adolf Hitler in a magazine with his mustache and his arm stretched out in a Nazi salute.

Janet thought he was wonderful. She liked the dictator's slicked-down hair and his mad, round eyes, and when she read about what he'd done, trying to conquer the world and exterminate the people he didn't like, she thought he seemed exactly like a god.

So she changed her name from Janet to Adolfa and bought a locket with a swastika engraved on it. Inside she put two greasy black curls, which an antique dealer had told her had been cut off Hitler's head when he was a baby. (He was lying, of course, but Adolfa was too far gone to notice.)

Next she joined something called CREEP. CREEP stood for the Council for the Re-Education of the English People. The loonies who belonged to it wanted Britain to be run like a police state with everyone marching about in uniforms and being flogged if they didn't obey the rules. CREEP wanted to get rid of dogs because they made a mess, and they wanted to get rid of the queen because she kept talking about peace and goodwill, whereas what CREEP wanted was a blood-thirsty war to make Britain great. (They thought that wars were good for people.) There were a lot of other things that CREEP wanted to get rid of: old people, because they weren't any use, and pop concerts, and vegetarians. And like all people with mad ideas, they started by throwing bombs.

Adolfa was very good at this. She didn't mind if children were blinded or innocent people had their legs blown off. But throwing bombs is expensive, and soon Adolfa was promoted to go and raise more money.

This was the reason she had come to America with her accomplices. For one of the ways of raising money is by kidnapping the children of rich people and holding them for ransom.

And who was richer, or loved his daughter more, than Hiram C. Hopgood of Granite Falls?

TRUCKS HAD BEEN arriving all day, unloading the square stones and round stones and pillars that had been Carra Castle. Then they drove away; darkness fell and the night watchman who guarded the site settled down in his hut by the road.

For an hour the heap of stones was silent. Then there was a rustle, a black muzzle appeared, and Cyril gave a short bark, which was at once hushed as a hairy hand came down on the dog's head.

But Cyril had woken the other ghosts. Stiff, their ectoplasm badly crumpled after the long journey, they rose and looked about them.

"Where are we?" asked Miss Spinks.

"Texas," said Krok. "It must be."

They gazed at Texas, which seemed to be a large field with a building on either side and a gas station opposite.

"Stars!" said Flossie, tilting her head upward and looking quite pleased for once.

But what she was gazing at were not stars. A necklace of lights was strung along the front of the Skyway Motel on their right. On the left, a winking blue crown hung on the roof of the Rex Cinema.

The ghosts were travel weary and confused. The thought that they were now American ghosts was hard to grasp.

"What do we do now?" Uncle Louse wanted to know. "Do we just go on haunting these stones or what?"

Krok frowned. "No, that wouldn't be right. We promised Alex we wouldn't haunt the castle. We must find somewhere else, but close enough to keep watch."

But Flossie couldn't take her eyes off the blue crown with the lights that came on and off. "Is it a palace?" she asked.

"A kind of palace," said Krok, who knew things. "A picture palace. They call it a cinema, too."

"Flossie wants to go into the palace," said the poltergeist.

"Not 'Flossie wants,'" said Miss Spinks wearily. "'I want.' Or rather, 'Please, may I—'"

It was at this moment that there came from the Rex Cinema the most delicious noise. A bloodcurdling scream, followed by hollow laughter . . . and then another scream even more bloodcurdling than the last.

The ghosts looked at one another and smiled. It was years since they had heard such a pleasant sound. Did it mean perhaps that there were other hideous phantoms nearby? That they might, here in America, find friends?

"We'll go and have a look," decided Krok.

So they made themselves invisible again and, calling Cyril to heel, they glided across the car park and into the cinema itself.

Inside it was dark, but far from empty. Rows and rows of people sat with their faces tilted upward at the screen—and on the screen itself were the loveliest things you could imagine!

First, the ghosts saw an overgrown grave in a churchyard. Then, rising from the grave . . . a vampire! A crazed vampire in human form with great long teeth and an evil leer!

By great good luck they had come in at the end of a horror film!

Uncle Louse couldn't take his eyes off the screen. It might have been him in his younger days—the mad vampire now flitting in through the lighted window of a house . . . entering the bedroom, sinking his teeth into the throat of the beautiful girl who lay there fast asleep.

"Aaagh!" screeched the girl, waking up, and leaped from the bed to escape the frightful creature. But the vampire was faster than she was . . . it raced after her . . . it pinned her against the wall.

"That's me!" whispered Uncle Louse, terribly excited. "The spit and image while I still had my teeth!" (This wasn't quite true. All Uncle Louse had done was take a sip or two from the maids as they slept, and they were strong, sensible girls who mostly didn't even wake up. But when you are old you remember things differently.)

Only Cyril wasn't staring at the screen, and that was because he had found something better—feet! Cyril liked many things: drains and bones and sausages, but there was nothing he liked better than hot and richly scented human feet. And here were rows and rows of them—feet smelling of horse dung and feet smelling of dust . . . feet smelling of gravy, and of other, lesser dogs—and feet just smelling truly and deeply of feet. Up and down the rows went Cyril, his nostrils flaring, while the people just sat there and never knew that a hellhound had passed them by.

But on the screen, things were going badly for the poor vampire. Some dreary detectives had come and dangled garlic in front of its nose, making it go all shivery and pale, and then they drove a stake through its heart and left it there, twitching. Uncle Louse was terribly upset, but films do sometimes end sadly, and there is nothing to be done. The silly woman that the vampire had been feeding on kissed one of the detectives, and then the curtains swished together and all Cyril's interesting feet started to move toward the door. Next came the ushers to make sure that nothing was left on the seats, and then a man put bars across the exits and turned out the lights, leaving the Rex Cinema dark—but not deserted.

It was then that Krok had his good idea.

"You know, I think we could do worse than stay here for the time being. The walls are strong, there's no chance of a sudden attack," he said, for Vikings are always worried about being ambushed in their sleep. "We'd be able to keep an eye on the castle, and there's plenty of room to stretch out between the seats and no one to worry us."

"But where could I drown myself?" asked Miss Spinks, who had got very dry on the journey.

"There'll be sinks in the restroom," said Krok. "Go and have a look."

Miss Spinks drifted off and came back looking much more cheerful, with dripping hair.

"Yes, you're right. There are sinks and a drinking fountain, too."

Uncle Louse was still upset about the vampire, but he, too, agreed—and so it was that the Rex Cinema became the ghosts' new home.

ALEX WAS ENJOYING HIMSELF at Green Meadows. Mr. Hopgood couldn't have been kinder, and Alex found himself liking and respecting Helen more with every day that passed. So it annoyed him the way Nurse Boniface bullied her and the way the whole house seemed to be turned into a kind of hospital.

"Why do you let them feed you all those pills?" asked Alex. "Red pills, green pills, blue pills—your poor stomach; it must be like a jumble sale in there."

Helen smiled, but her dark eyes were troubled. "They're supposed to make me better."

"Better from what? You're not *ill*. Why don't you just refuse to take them? Are you scared of Nurse Boniface?"

"Well, she's kind of fierce. But I suppose what I'm scared of more is upsetting my father. She only does what he tells her."

"Look, what your father wants is for you to get strong. Why don't you chuck the things away for a week, then if you get worse you'll know the pills have done you good, and I'll eat humble pie."

"Or a haggis?" said Helen, grinning.

Helen couldn't throw all the pills away because often Nurse Boniface stood over her to see if she swallowed them, but whenever she could, she buried them in a pot of geraniums. Alex was right, she didn't feel worse, she felt better.

Helen was allowed to swim—the doctors said it wouldn't hurt her—but at first she wouldn't bathe with Alex because she was embarrassed about her limp.

When Alex found out what was worrying her, he got angry. "Look, if we're going to Patagonia, you'll have to stop all this nonsense about exactly how long your left leg is. I simply can't be bothered with it. By the time we get there my nose might have been bitten off by a condor or anything. Good Lord, Krok's got three toes missing and his right ear is—"

He broke off, flushing. The last things to mention in Green Meadows were his ghosts.

So they went swimming and actually Helen swam very well. After Alex had splashed Nurse Boniface a few times "by accident," she went away and left them in peace.

At the end of the first week, Mr. Hopgood asked Alex if he'd like to go riding. There was a ranch not far away where they rented out horses.

Alex was really excited by the idea. He'd scrambled about on Highland ponies, but there'd been no money for proper riding. To ride here in Texas, perhaps with cowboys, was the best thing he could hope for.

"Can Helen come?" he asked Mr. Hopgood.

"Sure. She can't ride, of course—and it'll mean taking a bodyguard along—but she can watch."

The ranch was in open country, quite high up, and the horses were marvelous: lean, rangy beasts with wise eyes. A man called Rafe, in blue dungarees, put Alex up on a palomino. The saddle had a high pommel just like a Western. Alex started on a leading rein, but soon he was trotting around the paddock on his own, and then cantering.

But after an hour, he said something to Rafe and dismounted, and Rafe led the horse to where Helen was watching.

"You'd like a go, your friend says?"

Helen nodded, hardly daring to speak. She was lifted up, and though Rafe only walked her quietly up and down, she was riding like an ordinary girl!

"Well, how did you get on?" asked Mr. Hopgood that night.

"It was great!" said Alex. "Helen rode, too."

Mr. Hopgood put down his napkin. "Helen! Good God, boy, she might have fallen and crushed her leg." He was quite pale and his hand began to shake.

"But she didn't," said Alex cheerfully.

Mr. Hopgood was about to storm and make a scene, but then he looked at his daughter. Since Alex had come, Helen was a different girl.

After that, the children went riding most days, and as they drove past the building site, they could see how fast the work on the castle was getting on. Already, the foundations were dug, there were cranes and bulldozers everywhere, and you could see the layout quite clearly.

"It doesn't seem right that we should live there when it's been in your family so long," said Helen.

But Alex said it didn't matter; things changed. "I've kept Sethsay—that's an island off Carra Point—and I'd as soon be there as anywhere else in the world. There are white beaches and seals that sing when the weather's misty. And anyway, it won't be long until we're off to Patagonia."

It wasn't himself that Alex worried about, not for a minute. But though he was having such a good time, he couldn't help worrying night and day about his ghosts. *If only I knew they were all right,* he thought now. *If only they weren't so far away—thousands and thousands of miles away across the sea.*

That was what Alex was thinking as they drove past the Rex Cinema toward the Three Star Ranch.

Most of the workmen on the building site were happy to have a well-paid job. They worked hard and sang and cracked jokes, and at lunchtime they went into the huts and drank beer and ate sandwiches.

But two of the workmen were not happy.

Oscar the Hulk did not like wheeling heavy wheelbarrows with bags of cement in them. He got blisters on his hands and he got sweaty and he got tired. Pretending to be Madame Zugorsky, wearing a blond wig and wobbling about on high heels, had been all right, but Oscar had no use at all for hard work.

"I don't see why we don't just grab the brat and collect the ransom and go back home," he grumbled to Ratty Banks. "If anything goes wrong, we can always kill her and find another one. America's stuffed with millionaires."

Adolfa had sent both of them to get jobs on the building site, but Ratty nearly didn't get taken on at all. The foreman had taken one look at all the places where Ratty's muscles *weren't* and said he didn't want him. But

Ratty had squeaked and begged and shown him a book he'd bought at the station bookstall called *The Guggenfelder Bodybuilder.* This was full of exercises that a wrestler called Bertie Guggenfelder had put together to help people develop their bodies, and the idea of Ratty getting to look like Mr. Guggenfelder (who'd won the Iron Torso Competition three years running) made the foreman laugh so much that he let Ratty stay.

Adolfa, meanwhile, had booked into the Skyway Motel. She pretended to have nothing to do with Oscar and Ratty, and the manager of the hotel thought she seemed a most respectable British lady with her lace-up shoes, her steel-rimmed spectacles, and her sensible coat and skirt. It was a good thing that he couldn't see her at night, kissing a picture of Adolf Hitler, or watch her as she took out the locket with his hair in it. Adolfa, stroking with a bitten forefinger what she thought were the dictator's curls, was not a pleasant sight.

It was a good thing, too, that he didn't know what she kept in locked boxes under her bed. A set of different wigs and disguises so that she could spy on the people in Green Meadows without being recognized; two fine coils of rope; some stocking face masks; a pair of Sonnenheim pistols . . . and a silver knife with a pearl-encrusted handle.

If the manager of the Skyway Motel had known what

she meant to do with that knife, he wouldn't just have chucked her out of the hotel, he'd have been sick.

When Oscar and Ratty had been on the building site for five days, they went to meet Adolfa at the Twinkle Hamburger Bar on the road that led out of Granite Falls to the West.

Adolfa was waiting for them, looking more like an old-fashioned schoolmistress than ever.

"I'll have two hamburgers, a large helping of chips, and a beer," said Oscar hungrily when the waitress came.

"No, you won't," said Adolfa. "You'll have *one* hamburger and a *small* helping of chips and no beer at all, and so will Ratty."

Then she poured out three glasses of water and stood up. "We will drink to CREEP," she said.

"CREEP," mumbled Oscar, looking miserable because he wanted a beer.

"CREEP," said Ratty—and almost fell across the table because he'd knotted his legs together in the Guggenfelder exercise for strengthening the muscles of the calves.

"Well?" said Adolfa, sitting down again and looking at them in a nasty way.

"What do you mean, 'Well?,' Adolfa?" asked the Hulk nervously. (He was a very *henpecked* Hulk.)

"I mean, well, what have you discovered, what have

you learned, what have you *done*?" said Adolfa, and opened the locket.

"Done?" said Oscar in a hurt voice. "Worked ourselves into a lather, got sunstroke, got cramp . . ."

"Got nasty blisters," squeaked Ratty.

"I'm not interested in all that. You were supposed to study the layout. To snoop. To pry. To find out something useful."

"We did," said Oscar. "All the time we snooped and pried, didn't we, Ratty? Only there isn't anything to discover. There's just this field and people putting up a building."

Adolfa lifted her finger from Hitler's curl. A few of the greasy hairs stuck to her bitten skin, and she put them back carefully with the rest.

"You know, I think there'd better *be* something to discover," she said slowly. "Yes, I really think so. And quite soon." She snapped the locket shut. "I mean, you wouldn't want me to get *unpleasant*. . . ."

THE GHOSTS HAD BEEN living in the cinema for several days.

It was an old building. When Granite Falls was just a frontier town, it had been a variety theater and it had hardly changed since then. There were storerooms behind the stage and lots of doors that led into oddly shaped corridors and plenty of cooling drafts that whistled up from the floorboards. The red plush seats were worn and shabby and the curtains over the screen were badly frayed.

All this made the ghosts feel much more at home than they would have in one of those modern cinemas that is just a centrally heated box. Not that there weren't disadvantages. The place was cleaner than they would have liked because ladies came each morning to vacuum and dust, so that the poor spiders never got a chance to make a proper web and the cockroaches were shooed away as soon as they showed their heads. But Cyril was happy with the feet, and there was no one to bully them, so it might have been a great deal worse.

And they *loved* the vampire film!

It came on twice every night and they became terribly fond of the vampire. From the moment the curtains swished back and the graveyard came on the screen, with the sinister fog swirling around the tombstones, the ghosts were riveted. It turned out that the poor vampire had been cursed, just like Krok, so that it *had* to suck blood, which made them very angry with the way the silly girls screamed and fussed whenever it bent over their beds. It also made Krok wonder if he should try to kill someone here in the cinema, so as to get up to Valhalla to eat hog meat.

"I could swoop down with my battle-ax and utter a horrible war cry," he said one night to Miss Spinks when the other ghosts had gone to sleep. "Somewhere near the back, perhaps? It's quite likely someone would die of fright, don't you think?"

Miss Spinks looked up at him through her wet eyelashes, trying not to show how sad she would be if he left to go to Valhalla. "Of course, when you swoop and whoop you are absolutely terrifying," she agreed. "The trouble is, you might kill a *lot* of people. Women with weak hearts and so on. Would that be quite right?"

Krok thought about this. "Vikings did kill women, of course. They killed everybody, and who knows what their hearts were like? But it's true that I would rather slay a warrior. Perhaps, after all, I had better wait."

"I was wondering about Uncle Louse," said Miss Spinks, lowering her voice, for the old man was sleeping in his wheelchair above their head. "He's been so unsettled, seeing the film and remembering the old days. And I've heard that American dentists are very good. Do you think they might make him a set of teeth? Pointed ones? A little fanglike?"

This seemed to Krok to be a kind thought and, for a moment, he wondered if he should call the governess "Lettice." But then he decided this was going too far, so he said, "It is possible. But would they become part of him now that he has been dead so long? Are false teeth truly ghostly?"

It was a difficult question. "Alex would have known," said Miss Spinks, and both specters sighed. Missing Alex was an ache that never left them.

When *The Curse of the Vampire* had been on for five days, a dreadful thing happened. The film changed!

The ghosts were all hanging comfortably in their favorite place in front of the projection box when the curtains swished back, and instead of the lovely, creepy churchyard with the fog and the open grave, there was an orchard full of pink apple trees. Then the title appeared, and it was *Blossom Time*!

Next, a girl in a peasant dress came on. She started to milk a cow and sing a sickening song full of "tra la las." Then a man in leather shorts popped out from behind a tree and said he was going to Vienna to be a great composer, and then *he* sang, too.

As the awful film went on, the ghosts simply couldn't believe their eyes. There wasn't one scream, not one decent fight, not a single drop of blood! Although there was a perfectly good river in Vienna, not one person drowned in it; no one fell off the church steeples or got stabbed in an alleyway. All they did was sing, and when they didn't sing, they kissed.

"I don't think this is at all suitable for Flossie," said Miss Spinks anxiously.

But she needn't have worried. Flossie had taken one look at the girl with the cow and fallen asleep in midair, her thighbone in her mouth.

The ghosts, of course, had gone each day to see how the building of Carra was getting on. Usually they went after dark so that they didn't have to be invisible, but

Blossom Time made them feel so gloomy that they glided off the following morning.

It was an exciting sight that met their eyes! There were trucks backing and bulldozers shoveling and men banging at scaffolding or digging deep down in the foundations where the dungeons were to be. They had even started to excavate a place for the well!

"Oh, how beautiful it will look—oh, dear, dear Carra!" cried the governess, getting all emotional.

But that night, as Flossie was lying drowsily between Row L and Row M, which was where she liked to sleep, she said, "Flossie saw the lady with the coming-off bosoms."

Miss Spinks was very upset. She exchanged a glance with Krok, who had come to tell the poltergeist her bedtime story. It was so important for little children not to grow up rude and interested in things of that sort.

"Flossie, I don't want to hear any more words like that from you. And you *must* learn to say 'I' instead of 'Flossie.'"

"I—Flossie *did* see that lady. She had the coming-off bosoms and she had a wheelbarrow and she had hairy legs like Uncle Krok's."

"Don't be silly, dear. That lady was on the boat."

"No, she wasn't. She was here and—"

"Be silent, child!" thundered Krok. Viking children

never mentioned bosoms, and he was as upset as Miss Spinks.

But Flossie had turned purple with temper. She threw her bone across the seats and got up and began to stamp her feet as hard as she could. "Flossie did, she did, she did," screamed the poltergeist. And as she stamped and she screamed, she let off the full force of her racketing spirit.

Flossie had been good since they left Carra. She'd thrown a few antlers around at Dunloon and sent a few hats tumbling overboard on the *Queen Anne*. But now she really let rip! The ice-cream trays piled up in the corner rose and crashed down onto the aisle. The curtains across the screen billowed as if in a high wind and drew apart. A chandelier crashed to the ground—and everywhere in the cinema the doors flew open.

Flossie was good with doors. There was no door, however solidly built or locked or bolted, that she couldn't make fly open—it was one of her best tricks. The barred exits to the corridors flew open; so did the door to the projection room and to the foyer and the cloakrooms. And a very ancient iron door at the back of the stage . . . a door that no one had used, or even thought of, for years and years and years.

Flossie's temper tantrum blew itself out. She fell asleep, and presently the other ghosts slept also.

But in the dead, small hours, something appeared through the ancient, rusty door. A *hand* . . .

The Hand was by itself. It was severed—cut off at the wrist from its owner, who had been foully murdered a hundred years before. Since then, the Hand had lived alone in a maze of tunnels and caves deep below the Rex Cinema. It was a strong hand, and manly, but it was shy. Now, though, it groped its way between the rows of seats, sometimes walking on tiptoe, on its fingers, sometimes looping along like a caterpillar, and as it walked or looped, it glowed with a soft blue light that shone through its bloodied fingernails and lit up the shattered bone and muscle of its wrist.

The Hand had never been in the cinema. It had never been through the door that Flossie had blown open, but it felt that somewhere nearby there were beings like itself, beings that might understand it and know how difficult it was to be severed, and alone, and underground. And it felt that it would be nice to leave them a message.

The Hand could not speak too well because it had no mouth, but it could write. There was no difficulty about what to write *on*—the large white screen was perfect. But what to write *with*? The Hand had come up from below without a pencil or a pen. For a while it wandered between the seats, moving its thumb back and forward in a puzzled way. Then, suddenly, it pounced. It had found a golden tube about the length of its own little finger. (Just as it had learned to glow through years of living in darkness, and to think with the nerves that were left to it, so the Hand had learned to make out simple shapes even without eyes.)

What the Hand had found was a lipstick—a deep crimson one, the color of blood. Very pleased, it unscrewed the top and clambered up the side of the screen.

Then it paused because it wanted to get the message *right*: simple and friendly, but sincere.

After a while it wrote:

WELCOME FROM THE HAND

Then it walked on fingertips all over the message to feel how it had come out, and after another pause, it added "SEVERED" after "HAND," because it wanted to make it clear that it wasn't just any old hand.

Now the message said:

WELCOME FROM THE HAND (SEVERED)

After this, the Hand suddenly felt very tired, and it clambered down and looped back through the iron door behind the screen, through an old and dusty storeroom, down a flight of dank stone steps, through a cobwebby corridor, and on, down and down, into the dark.

For the Rex Cinema, though few people knew it, was a much more complicated building than it seemed.

THE FRIENDSHIP BETWEEN Alex and Helen grew steadily. Helen had buried nearly three hundred pills in the potted geranium, and though the plant was beginning to look droopy, Helen was not. She now went riding with Alex and swimming with him, and at night they planned their expedition to Patagonia. That wild country at the tip of South America was becoming very real to them: the lakes on which flamingos swam, the grassy valleys studded with flowers, and the mountains with their ice-blue peaks. Neither of them doubted that they would find the giant sloth, but they argued about what to do when they did find it. Alex wanted to bring it back and show it to the world in a really good zoo. Helen wanted to photograph it and leave it where it was.

Mr. Hopgood, like Helen, was getting very fond of

Alex, but Nurse Boniface hated the Scottish boy. She felt that he was taking her patient away from her and that she'd soon be out of a job, and she was right. For once someone young has really decided to get well, they usually do, and Helen could hardly remember how frightened and hopeless she had felt before Alex came.

Meanwhile, Carra was growing and growing. The four towers were halfway to their full height, the gateway was nearly finished, and work on the drawbridge had begun.

"Is everything as it should be?" Mr. Hopgood asked Alex as the foreman took them around the building.

"Yes, it is. It's all absolutely correct," said Alex—but Mr. Hopgood caught a slight doubt in his voice.

"What is it, boy? Remember, I want the place just the way it was, so don't be afraid to speak."

"Well, it's just that everything looks so *clean*," said Alex. "You see, from being so old, Carra was full of . . . oh, slime and bird droppings and owl pellets. And there were cobwebs and bats and . . . just dust, I suppose. Of course, I see that you can't have that here."

"What do you mean, I can't have it here?" said Mr. Hopgood, nettled. "I work hard enough—if I want dust and slime and bird droppings, then dust and slime and bird droppings I will have."

So that night they drew up a shopping list, and the following morning the three of them drove to Searly and Rowlock, the most famous department store in Texas.

It was an amazing place. If Alex hadn't known they were in a shop, he'd have thought they were in a maharaja's palace. The carpets were ankle-deep, perfume wafted through the air; there were real fountains and flowering camellia trees in tubs.

And the things that were for sale!

There were fur coats made of Russian sable, and dresses of wild silk sewn with pearls, and satin nightshirts trimmed with silver braid. In the food hall, live swordfish and exotic eels swam in a great aquarium, and if you pointed to one of them, an assistant came and caught it and hit it on the head and filleted it for you then and there. There were trash cans covered in real mink and ovens that played "The Star-Spangled Banner" when the food was cooked—and a tray of little gold discs with HIS and HERS written on them in diamonds, which had Alex completely flummoxed.

"What on earth are those?" he asked.

"They're for people to wear in their tummy buttons as they lie beside their swimming pools," explained Helen.

Alex was shocked. Mr. Hopgood worked so hard and looked so worried that it hadn't seemed particularly wrong that he should be so rich. But people labeling their tummy buttons to show which of them was which, or keeping the rubbish warm with mink when in other countries children were starving, just couldn't be right.

"It's a bit like Dunloon," he said to Helen. "That's the place I told you about where my mother's cousin lives, Lady Trottle. It's full of stuff that's valuable, but absolutely useless, like snuffboxes and the bed socks of dead kings."

Just then there was a sudden scuffle at the next counter, and a lady with red hair reared up and dislodged a rhinoceros-hide wastepaper basket, which fell over her head, snuffing her out like a candle.

But before anyone could go to help her, a hand with bitten-looking fingers came up and lifted the basket off, and the lady, whose hair now looked very lopsided, scuttled toward the exit.

Adolfa (because that's who it was, of course) had heard something most useful and important. She'd been snooping around Green Meadows for days and following the children, trying to work out how to get herself asked into the house, and now she knew how to do it.

For Adolfa had been to Dunloon! A long time ago, it was true, when she was still in the band with her sisters. The Beautiful Batters had been asked down to Dunloon to play at the Servants' Ball. Maisie Batters had got a bit sloshed and dropped her trombone in the goldfish tank, and when she came to play her solo, a little fish had shot out and landed on the butler's feet. Lady Trottle had thought this very funny, and Adolfa remembered her well.

All she had to do was to pretend that she had a message for Alex from his mother's cousin. Then they'd *have* to invite her to Green Meadows, and once she was inside, she'd certainly find some way of getting herself asked to the Opening Ball at the castle.

And Adolfa's eyes, as she scuttled from the store, glittered with triumph.

Meanwhile, Mr. Hopgood and the children had reached the pet department. They could see an armadillo in a cage and two baboons with interesting-looking behinds, but there didn't seem to be any of the things on their list.

"Three hundred spiders," read the young assistant. He looked up, frowning. "You mean black widow spiders, perhaps, sir? The kind whose bite means instant death? Or tarantulas, who make one go insane?"

"No, I don't," said Mr. Hopgood. "I mean ordinary household spiders. And I mean ordinary cockroaches, too, and ordinary jackdaws, just like it says."

The assistant sighed. "Ordinariness is not something we go in for at Searly and Rowlock. Now if you wanted a Bactrian camel, we could deliver it to your door within the week. Or the other kind without the extra hump. No problem at all, that would be."

"Well, I don't," said Mr. Hopgood shortly. "I want exactly what it says on the list, and I want it by the first week in December."

"I shall have to consult the manager," said the young man.

Mr. Hopgood now got angry and made a fuss, as only a millionaire can do, and the manager came and swore that every single thing on the list would be delivered to Granite Falls by the seventh of December. "All of it, sir—the bats, the slime, the raven for the roof. Even if we make a loss on the deal, even if we have to scour the length and breadth of our great land," he promised, pumping Mr. Hopgood's hand.

"Well, that's that," said Mr. Hopgood as they came out of the store. "I reckon by the time we're through, Carra will look just the way it did back in Scotland."

"I tell you what we didn't order, though," said Helen as they made their way toward the parking lot.

"What's that, honey?" asked Mr. Hopgood.

She smiled. "A ghost!"

Alex looked up quickly, his face full of hope. Could he, after all, let the Hopgoods into Carra's secret? But Mr. Hopgood's face wore its anxious look again.

"Now, Helen, don't be foolish. As if I'd ever let a ghost near my little girl to frighten her! Even if there were such things."

And Alex sighed and said no more.

"Would you like another sandwich?" Helen Hopgood asked politely, and turned her head away because Miss Batters eating the thin rolled-up asparagus sandwiches that Maria had prepared was not a pleasant sight. Miss Batters had arrived in gloves, but she had removed them, of course, for tea, and her forefinger was so badly bitten that the torn skin caught on the bread in a most unpleasant way.

Altogether, both the children found it impossible to like Miss Batters. Though she looked so respectable, with her gray cropped hair and her steel-rimmed spectacles, there was something about her that bothered them. Perhaps it was the way she fiddled with her locket, as though it held something she wanted to stroke and touch; perhaps it was the way her old-fashioned lace-up shoes bulged at the sides, as though she had put her bunions in a straitjacket. But, of course, when she had telephoned to say that Lady Trottle had asked her to look up Alex, there'd been nothing to do except ask her to tea.

"It's such a beautiful, beautiful place, dear Dunloon," said Adolfa, while her sludge-colored eyes darted around

the room, noticing everything. She'd been right to postpone the snatch until they moved to the castle. It had taken her ten minutes to get from the front gate in here.

"Yes, I suppose it is," said Alex. He hardly remembered Dunloon, but there was no point in disagreeing with Miss Batters.

But what Adolfa really wanted to know was the plan for moving into the castle, and she now brought the conversation around to the Opening Ball. If Mr. Hopgood had been there, he might have smelled a rat, but Alex and Helen answered her freely enough. Adolfa seemed such an awful-looking woman, her bitten forefinger was so nasty, and her imprisoned bunions looked so depressing that Helen said, "Would you like me to ask my father if you could come? Then you could tell Lady Trottle about it afterward."

Adolfa put down her cup and her thin lips twisted into a smile of satisfaction.

"Thank you, my dear. That would be very, very kind. I'm only a lonely visitor to this country without friends and relations, and that would really be something to look forward to."

Just then, Nurse Boniface came to fetch Helen because the physical therapist had arrived and, for a moment, Alex and Miss Batters were alone.

"I was wondering," he said hurriedly, "when you

were at Dunloon, did you, by any chance, see any ghosts? Not the Green Lady or the Red Lady, but proper ones? A phantom dog, perhaps . . . or a Viking?"

Adolfa backed away from him, her eyes bulging with horror. Was he joking? If there was one thing that absolutely nauseated her, it was anything unreal or weird. She could throw bombs and see people screaming with pain—but ghosts . . . Ugh!

"No, indeed I didn't," she said sharply. "Quite honestly, I think that jokes should not be made on subjects like that."

And Adolfa grabbed her gloves and her hat and hurried away.

But that night, Alex wrote a letter to Dunloon.

THE GHOSTS WERE very pleased with the message from the Hand.

"My, my, that's a very good class of hand," said Uncle Louse, who knew about these things. "There's nothing classier than being severed. It'll have a bloodstained wrist stump and get up to all sorts of tricks, I shouldn't wonder."

"It is good to be welcomed," said Krok. "Though it's strange that we have seen no signs of it. Its invisibility must be very high."

The ghosts were particularly glad of the Hand's message, because their spirits were becoming rather low. Awful *Blossom Time* was still showing twice daily, and because it was a film that was supposed to be suitable for children, there were a great many chewing-gum wrappers and lollipop sticks left behind that stuck to the ghosts' ectoplasm and made them itch. Being invisible so much of the time made them tired, and Cyril was so short of exercise that the stale air had got trapped in his long stomach and came out in bursts at either end, which worried him. They were also getting more and more bothered about how to get a message to Alex back in Scotland without appearing to Mr. Hopgood, which they had promised not to do.

What made everything worse, of course, was seeing Carra rise in all its glory so close to them. The East Tower, their own familiar place, was halfway built; they could see the torture chamber quite clearly, and the dungeons where they had picnicked so happily were almost underneath them in the parking lot of the cinema.

"It may simply hurt too much to live so close to Carra and be forbidden to enter it," said the Viking. "We must see it rebuilt, of course, but after that perhaps we should move on and put the past behind us."

"We could do that, I suppose," said Uncle Louse. "Become prairie ghosts. There must be Indian spooks out there, and plenty of them."

But he spoke very sadly. At his age he did not think he would get on too well with ghosts that were called things like Big Knee Joint and wore feathers on their heads.

A few days later the ghosts found another message from the Hand. It said:

ALL IS NOT WHAT IT SEEMS
(Signed) THE HAND

The ghosts found this very interesting, and it was decided to keep a watch for the Hand and welcome it in person. Since Krok was the strongest and best able to do without sleep, it was he who stayed up and waited.

The first night there was no sign of anything unusual, nor the second. But on the third, a pale blue glow appeared around the corner of the screen . . . stopped . . . came on again . . . and Krok saw the Hand's fine, upside-down fingers coming toward him, crowned with the bloodied bones and muscle of the wrist.

Actually, the Hand had nearly stayed away because the ghosts had made Flossie shut all the doors she had opened in her temper tantrum, and it had not been at all sure whether it could go through solid wood or metal. The way you learn what you are is by people telling you, and there had been no one to tell the Hand whether it was a ghost or not. But when it had pressed itself a few times against the rusty door that led into the storeroom behind the stage, it found that it had passed through to the other side.

Knowing that it was not only severed but ghostly cheered the Hand very much. All the same, when a deep voice boomed at it suddenly out of the darkness of the cinema, the Hand nearly jumped out of its skin, and the lipstick it was carrying under one finger clattered to the floor.

"Greetings, O Severed hand," said Krok.

The Hand gathered up its courage. Bravely it moved forward and climbed across a pair of thonged sandals, up a leather trouser leg, across a chain shirt, and into a rough and curly beard. Then it laid its fingers across the speaker's mouth and waited.

"Greetings, O Severed Hand," repeated Krok, for he understood that the Hand, not having ears, liked to *feel* what people said.

The Hand nodded with one finger, climbed quickly down again, picked up the lipstick, and hurried over to the screen.

"Greetings, O Mighty Warrior," it wrote.

They were not introduced. To the Hand, who had lived alone in murk and gloom so long, finding someone to tell things to was happiness indeed, and very quickly and excitedly it wrote the story of its life.

"In 1881," wrote the Hand, "I was still joined to a man named Arthur Brett who came from England to find gold. Most of the people who took part in the gold rush went to California, but Arthur found that there were small amounts of gold here in Texas. He went into partnership with a man called Erik Erikson and they started a mine. But Erikson was a crook. He wanted all the gold for himself, and one day he murdered Arthur by pushing him under a trolley. The wheels went over Arthur's wrist so that I became severed from him. Why I stayed and became ghostly and the rest of Arthur did not, I don't know. These things are very mysterious. Since then, I have lived by myself in the mine, which is dark and flooded and, to be honest, I have sometimes been very lonely and sad. Though one must not grumble."

Krok was very interested in all this and very sorry for the Hand.

"But where is the mine?" he asked, bending down very low so that the Hand could lip-read.

"It is underneath the cinema," replied the Hand, writing with its lipstick. "Reached by a tunnel from behind the storeroom. It is a dreadful place, but you are welcome to visit."

Krok was amazed. A mine so close! Yet now that he thought of it, the cracks in the wall of the building, the mysterious passages leading nowhere, should have warned him that there was more to the Rex Cinema than met the eye.

"Why don't you come and live with us here?" Krok wanted to know.

"Thank you, but I must stay and avenge the murder of Arthur Brett," wrote the Hand.

By this time the lipstick was worn down almost to its stump, and the Hand, exhausted by so much communication, crept away.

The other ghosts were very excited by what Krok had to tell them, and when the Hand came back two days later, they were all waiting to welcome it.

Everybody liked it at once. Flossie loved the blue glow it made and wanted to keep it for a night-light. Uncle Louse was delighted with its excellent manners, for it climbed at once onto his lap and bowed, bending all its fingers from the knuckles in a most courtly and old-fashioned way.

Only Cyril was at first puzzled, not being sure whether it was something to bark at or to chase, or to back away from in terror, but when he had done all these, he suddenly shot out his forked tongue and began to lick the Hand all over.

There is nothing that tickles more than being licked by a hellhound, but though the Hand couldn't help quivering and shaking, it made no attempt to get away. It was as though it knew that what was happening was important.

And when Cyril had finished, the ghosts were quite awed by how handsome their new friend looked now that the grime and muck of a hundred years was washed away. The blue veins ran like little rivers across its skin;

the half-moons at the base of the nails were beautifully shaped, and what they had thought was a piece of string tied around the little finger turned out to be a signet ring stamped with Arthur Brett's initials.

"You can see it comes from a good family," murmured Miss Spinks—and turning as she always did to Krok, she whispered, "Do you think we might ask it to write a letter for us to Alex in Scotland? It writes such a beautiful script."

Krok thought this was an excellent idea. A letter like that could go through the ordinary post—they could have a reply in no time. He repeated what Miss Spinks had said to the Hand, who seized the lipstick stump and almost ran to the screen.

"I would be delighted. Charmed. More pleased than I can say," it wrote. "To be a Helping Hand as well as a Severed Hand would make me completely happy. Or rather as happy as I can be until I have avenged the murder of Arthur Brett."

So it was decided that the Hand should come back next day when the ghosts had got some writing paper and stamps from the manager's office. Miss Spinks also suggested that they should stop calling the Hand "it" and call it "he" because it was so manly and strong.

The Hand, who was getting very good at lipreading, was tremendously pleased. An "it" is a *thing*, but a "he" is a *person*—and as he made his way back to the mine, he moved lightly, almost as if he were dancing—as people do when they have found friends.

But at the end of the week, a cleaning lady called Millie Jones who worked in the cinema handed in her notice. She said she was sick of rubbing a lot of gibberish off the screen with lipstick remover, and she got a job in a launderette instead.

ALEX'S LETTER WAS brought to Lady Trottle on a silver salver, and it surprised her, because Alex, like most boys, had never been too keen on letter writing.

She was alone at the time. Dunloon was so expensive to run that the Trottles had run out of money, and Sir Ian had gone to London to try to borrow some more from a bank.

Alex had written:

Dear Aunt Dorothy,

I arrived safely in America and I'm having a very nice time here. Mr. Hopgood is most hospitable, and the rebuilding of Carra is going well. But the thing is, I'm a bit worried about my ghosts. Your friend Adolfa Batters came to tea today and gave me all sorts of kind messages, but she didn't seem to know anything about them. I've never felt right about asking them to go away—not that they wouldn't be fine at Dunloon, but you know how it is. Has Cyril settled down? Is Flossie behaving herself? If you could just send me a few lines to say they're all right, I'd be most grateful.

Thank you very much.
Your affectionate cousin,
Alex

Lady Trottle put down the letter and *thought*. This was not a thing she did often, but she could do it if she tried. Then she rang for the butler and said, "Phillips, have you seen any of the new ghosts lately? The ones from Carra?"

"No, my lady; I have not. I'm happy to say there have been no more floating bed socks or governesses in Sir Ian's bath."

"It's strange that they should suddenly have gone so quiet. What about our own ghosts?"

The butler said he hadn't noticed them of late. "But, of course, our own ghosts do not give any trouble."

"Well, let me know if you see any of them. I've had a letter from my young cousin, the MacBuff of Carra."

Two days later, the butler came to say that the Green Lady and the Red Lady had been seen in the linen cupboard, and Lady Trottle went up to find them. Both specters, when they saw her, attempted to vanish, but when she wished to, Lady Trottle could be firm.

"No, you don't," she said. "I want to talk to you. Where's Hal?"

Handsome Hal appeared, waveringly. He, too, looked uneasy.

"I want to know what's happened to the Carra ghosts," asked Lady Trottle. "They were here a few weeks ago because I saw them. But there's been no sighting since and I'd like to know why."

The Green Lady looked at the Red Lady and then both Ladies looked at Hal.

"The Carra ghosts did not fit in," said the Red Lady at last. "We tried to show them how things were done in an aristocratic household, but they seemed to be quite unable to learn."

Lady Trottle frowned. "This happens to be my home," she said, "and I gave them sanctuary. You will kindly tell me where they are now."

"We don't know," said the Green Lady, fanning herself.

"Stop whirring that fan at me," said Lady Trottle. "What do you mean, you don't know?"

"We didn't see them go. They just went. The day after—"

She broke off as Hal gave a warning, spectral cough.

"The day after what?" said Lady Trottle sharply.

"We were forced to discipline the dog . . . after dear Sir Ian sat on the dead ferret."

Lady Trottle's lips twitched into a smile. Her husband often annoyed her, and she had enjoyed seeing him leap up from the sofa with pieces of dead ferret stuck to his behind.

"How did you discipline him?"

"We sent him to the cowshed. And after that, the ghosts just vanished. It was extremely rude of them. They didn't say good-bye, and the Viking left a throwing spear that is no use to anyone. I fell over it on the way to my closet."

Lady Trottle was worried by this news. She felt that she had failed in hospitality. "You're quite certain they're not just somewhere being invisible?"

The Ladies nodded.

"Well, then I'm very displeased with you. Very displeased indeed. The Carra ghosts were your guests. Their home has been pulled down; they have nowhere to go; heaven knows what has happened to them. You'd better keep out of my sight or I'll have you exorcised."

The ghosts were quiet until Lady Trottle had gone, but then they began to titter with glee and to mock and to jeer.

"Their home has been pulled down, did you hear that!"

"They have nowhere to go!"

"They'll be haunting some Scottish pigsty and serve them right!"

Lady Trottle went downstairs, much disturbed, and wrote at once to Alex, explaining what had happened.

> I think they must have gone back to Carra and be haunting somewhere near there. I'll have inquiries made—and I'm really very sorry, my dear boy. As soon as they're found, I'll invite them back personally and keep my own ghosts in order. As for Adolfa Batters, I don't know who she can be. I don't know anyone called that, and one could hardly forget such a strange Christian name. Perhaps she's got me mixed up with the Trottles of Farmlington—my husband's brother and his wife—though they wouldn't be likely to send messages to you!

Lady Trottle finished her letter and sealed it. She even put on a stamp. But then she left it lying in the muddle of papers on her bureau, so it did not reach Alex until weeks later, when a maid found it and posted it. So Alex went on trusting Adolfa and believing what she said, and for this he was to blame himself horribly later.

RATTY AND OSCAR had been reporting every few days to Adolfa in the Twinkle Hamburger Bar. They had never been allowed more than one hamburger and they had never been allowed a beer. But the week after Adolfa went to tea at Green Meadows, they hurried into the restaurant and both of them were gibbering with excitement.

"Well," said Adolfa, who was as usual stroking Hitler's curl.

"We've discovered something, Adolfa," said the Hulk.

"*I* discovered it," squeaked Ratty, who was sitting on Mr. Guggenfelder's book, *Bodybuilding Exercises,* to make himself look taller. "Not you; I did! When we were down in the dungeons laying the underground cables." He lowered his voice and leaned across the table, whispering in a hot and agitated voice.

"Are you sure?" asked Adolfa when he had finished.

"I'm quite sure. Absolutely certain. Some of the older men knew about it. It's been disused for years, but it's there."

"So now can we have a beer?" asked the Hulk.

Adolfa ignored him. She put the curl to bed and shut the locket with a snap. "In that case," she said, "my plan is complete. Yes, I see my way now. Listen carefully, both of you: this is what I want you to do. . . ."

As the weeks passed, the people of Granite Falls became more and more excited as this genuine, proper Scottish castle rose in their midst.

Mr. Hopgood had announced that the great Opening Ball would be held on December 14. He had invited all the important people in Granite Falls and quite a lot of people who weren't "important" but simply nice, like the gas station attendant and the lady in the corner store who sold him the extra-strong peppermints he sucked to soothe his stomach. And even the people he couldn't invite would be able to see the castle floodlit in all its glory and hear the pipers as they marched around the battlements before the dancing began.

By the beginning of December no town could have been more Scottish than Granite Falls. The owner of the Skyway Motel took down the picture of the president that hung in his dining room and put up one of the queen at Balmoral stalking deer. The chef at the Twinkle Hamburger Bar invented a MacBuffburger made of minced kipper and oatmeal. And the manager of the Rex Cinema decided to have an all-night showing of Scottish films at the same time as the ball, with the ushers dressed in tartan, and special sweets like licorice bagpipes and sporrans made of toffee to serve in the intervals.

Meanwhile, the ghosts were holding a meeting.

"Are we agreed, then?" asked Krok.

Miss Spinks, fresh from the drinking fountain, nodded sadly, sending a shower of drops over Cyril, who looked at her reproachfully out of his saucer eyes.

"It will not be so bad, perhaps?" sighed Uncle Louse. "They can't all be called Big Knee Joint or Wise Toe Nail. There might be some quite ordinary ghosts called Cynthia or Fred."

"And there might be little papoose spooks for Flossie to play with," said Miss Spinks—and the poltergeist, who was drawing a picture of the Big Blob with a melting chocolate bar on one of the seats, let out an Indian war whoop in her piping voice.

The ghosts had decided to leave the cinema and go west. The pain of seeing Carra, now almost finished, so close to them and knowing that they could never again live there and call it home was too great to be borne. If they had heard from Alex, everything would have been different. To see Alex once more they would have lived in the cinema forever, but though the Hand had written a most beautiful letter and bravely gone out at night, looping along Main Street after everyone was in bed to mail it, there had been no answer. (This was because the Hand had not been out of the mine for a hundred years and did not realize how things had changed. Though he felt most carefully for something round with a slit in it, he had mailed the letter in a trash bin.)

"We will stay until the night of the Opening Ball," decided Krok. "Then at the stroke of midnight we will glide away westward across the prairie, and perhaps the Spirits of Doom and Darkness will grant us peace and a new home."

But what was to be done about the Hand?

They had asked him to the meeting and he had listened most carefully, climbing up and down to lip-read and not complaining, though so much exercise made him tired.

Now Uncle Louse said, "What about it, friend? Why don't you come with us? There's plenty of room in my chair for both you and Flossie."

The others all joined in, begging the Hand to leave the dark and lonely mine and come with them. You could see how tempted he was—sweat broke out on his palm just thinking about it. But then he picked up the pencil they had taken from the office, and the paper, and now as he wrote, the letters were not smooth and perfectly rounded but quavery and untidy, because he was telling them his most deep and personal thoughts.

"I have already told you how happy I was joined to Arthur Brett, who was a scholar and a gentleman and never spoke a cross word to me in the thirty-eight years we were together. You also know that I feel I must avenge his murder by the vile Erik Erikson, though I must say I do not see how to do this just at present. But there is something I have not told you." Here the Hand paused, and the ghosts were afraid that, after all, he did not wish to share his secret. But he picked up the pencil again and wrote, "And it is this: There are certain kinds of hand that are not only severed and ghastly, but also magical. When such a hand spreads its fingers, every single living thing is frozen into immobility—which means it stops dead still and cannot move or breathe or speak until the Hand allows it. A hand like this is called a Hand of Glory, and to become glorious in this way is what I want more than anything in the world. Every day in the quiet and darkness of the mine I practice and practice, but the exercises are difficult and I do not think they could be done in the open prairie among Indian ghosts who lead such different lives."

After this, the ghosts did not try to persuade him any-more. When someone has work to do, he must be al-lowed to get on and do it. All the same, they felt very sad. Considering how little there was of him, it was extraor-dinary how important the Hand had become to them.

On December 10 the flagpole was hammered into place on the gatehouse tower and the castle was complete.

It looked magnificent. Mr. Hopgood had asked Alex if he might fly the MacBuff flag with a golden eagle on a background of red and black, and Alex had said of course. All the furniture that had come over on the *Queen Anne* had been polished and mended, and Mr. Hopgood had bought other antiques, like pictures of stags fighting each other and wall hangings of Saint Sebastian being stuck full of arrows, which he thought would fit in well.

Searly and Rowlock had kept their promise. Delivery vans had arrived with crates full of spiders and cock-roaches and bats, and men had put up ladders and painted the walls with bird droppings and slime.

"Doesn't it look fantastic!" said Helen, quite over-come, as she and Alex followed Mr. Hopgood through the rooms. "If only you could stay and live here, too!"

But Alex couldn't and she understood this really. He was staying for the ball and he was going to spend their first Christmas with them in the castle, but after that he had to go home. Aunt Geraldine was alone in Torquay and he had promised to go and see the New Year in with her. And, of course, there was school. But what really drew him back was his homesickness for the ghosts. Not getting a reply from Dunloon had shaken Alex badly.

Two days before the ball, the caterers came, and the ladies to arrange the flowers, and the security people to guard the treasures and make sure that no one got in without an invitation.

And lastly, marching down Main Street in a swirl of kilts, came the Errenrig Pipe Band, which Mr. Hopgood had flown in specially from Scotland.

It was going to be the most splendid, the most exciting ball there had ever been.

17

DOWN IN THE DARKNESS of the mine, the Hand was trying to become glorious.

He had done his exercises, making his blue glow stronger and then weaker so as to give a sinister flickering effect, and spreading his fingers as if to say "STOP." But he was feeling unwell. Something wasn't right. There were clanking noises where for years there had been silence, broken only by the drip, drip of the water running down the rock face, or the plop of a loose pebble falling two hundred meters into the murky black pool that had been formed by floodwater at the bottom of one of the shafts.

"Every day and in every way I am getting gloriouser and gloriouser," wrote the Hand with an old piece of stick on the loose gravel. He wrote this ten times a day in the hope that soon he really would become a Hand of

Glory, but today his fingers trembled so much that there was no point in going on.

It's because the ghosts are going away, I expect, thought the Hand. *That's why I'm so upset.*

Clank! There it was again! He spread himself flat on the ground so as to let the noise pass through his bones and skin.

There was no doubt about it. The sound came from the ancient, rusty trolleys. Someone had set them going again. Perhaps even now the actual trolley that had killed Arthur Brett was rolling toward him!

I mustn't be like this, thought the Hand as it shivered and shook. *I must pull myself together or I'll never be a Hand of Glory.*

Should he go and investigate? It meant going through the wide place where the three tunnels met: his own, the one from the field where they'd built the castle, and the dreadful tunnel that led down to the bottomless pool. He was never happy in that part of the mine—if he lost his way and fell into the water, there was no hope for him.

The Hand's blue glow got fainter and fainter as he decided what to do. He could feel footsteps, too—slow, heavy ones. Whoever was thumping about must be a huge hulk of a man.

I could go and tell the ghosts in the cinema, he thought. A trouble shared is a trouble halved, Arthur always said.

But they were leaving the next day; it seemed wrong to go and upset them now. *And the ghosts looked up to me,* thought the poor Hand. *What would they say if they could see me shaking like a leaf?*

But now, suddenly, the Hand felt a new shock, a shock so dreadful that he tottered backward and all but fell. Every blood vessel in every finger throbbed and pounded with fear; even his chilblain tingled with terror.

Something new and different had entered the mine. A second set of footsteps—and with them a presence so evil and appalling that the Hand did not think he could survive it.

What can it be? thought the Hand, feeling himself choked by vileness. The wickedness seemed to stretch back into the past . . . to a time when he had not been severed, but led a carefree life playing the piano and scratching Arthur Brett behind the ear. Yes, what he felt now belonged to that unspeakable moment when the trolley had passed over Arthur's wrist and Erik Erikson had done the foulest, the most evil deed known to man—murder—and gone unpunished.

Erikson . . . that was what it was! The smell, the feel, the awfulness of Erik Erikson was everywhere. He could reach out and touch it.

Erikson, or his ghost, must be here down below . . .

quite close to him and coming closer! Erikson returned to visit the scene of his crime!

The Hand seized a piece of stick to scrawl a message of despair, but it clattered from his fingers. Then his knuckles gave way and he fell to the ground.

Overcome by the horror of it all, the Hand had fainted.

The great day had arrived and the people of Granite Falls were getting ready for the ball.

Mrs. Franklyn, the mayor's wife, fastened a dozen tartan ribbons into the curls of her conceited little daughter, Lillianne, who smirked and prinked in front of the mirror.

"I'll be the prettiest girl there, won't I, Ma?" said Lillianne, smiling to show her dimples.

"Of course, honey. But you must remember to be nice to poor Helen. Not everyone is as fortunate as you."

Mr. O'Leary, who ran the bowling alley, lowered his foot into his evening shoe and yowled with pain, because his wife had smashed his big toe when she was teaching him to dance an Eightsome Reel.

And everywhere there appeared—knees! Knees that hadn't been seen for years; knobbly ones and fat ones, warty ones and dimpled ones, as the citizens of Granite Falls put on their kilts.

Adolfa Batters, too, was getting ready for the ball. She had sprayed a scent called Purple Heather into her unpleasant armpits and now put on a ruffled tartan dress that made her look like a Highland ham in a butcher's shop. Then she flashed the locket with the swastika on it out from under her vest and arranged it on her scraggy chest, because she didn't want Hitler's curl to miss what was going on.

"I look like my great-great-grandfather in the painting," she said, gazing at herself smugly. Mr. Erik Erikson had led an interesting life with a lot of foreign travel before he settled in London. No one knew why he had changed his name to Batters, but Adolfa had always admired his picture in the dining room and thought he was just the sort of person to have done well in CREEP.

When she had finished dressing, she picked up a flashlight and went to the window.

A few minutes later, Oscar the Hulk appeared in the doorway. He wore a black hairpiece to cover his scar, and a black mustache, and looked even nastier than usual. There was an armband saying *Security* around his arm, and a badge in his lapel, and he wore a holster.

Adolfa nodded. It had been worth paying the Bulgoni brothers to get him false papers and set him up as a security guard. The Hulk had been taken on to watch over

Mr. Hopgood's treasures; he'd be able to get in and out of the castle with no questions asked.

"And the car?" she asked sharply.

Oscar nodded in the direction of the parking lot, where a red Ferrari waited. It had a special number plate and the words *Securicars, Inc.* were painted on the sides. The Bulgonis were expensive, but they did their stuff.

"Now go through your instructions," ordered Adolfa.

"I'm to wait until you've pushed the kid through the tunnel and Ratty's grabbed her. Then I'm to take the bits of clothes of hers you give me and drop them in the copse behind the Three Star Ranch for the police to find. Exactly at nine A.M. I'm to go to the phone box on the crossroads and phone the ransom demand. Then—"

"All right; that'll do. And Ratty?"

Oscar grinned. "He's waiting to go down through the cinema, but he's feeling sore. Says he'll get chilblains. He's put on a pair of woolen underpants and got himself some cough drops."

It was true. Ratty was feeling very sorry for himself. Oscar had all the fun, dressing up as a detective and laying false trails in flashy cars, while he had to stay down in the cold and the dark. But one day he'd show them, thought the little crook as he shuffled forward in the line for *Raiders of the Glen*. The way his bodybuilding exercises were going, he'd soon be as strong as any of them—and then they'd best watch out!

"Do I look all right?" asked Helen, turning from the mirror in her room in Green Meadows.

"You look fine," said Alex. "Don't fuss."

Helen wore a simple white dress, such as girls used to wear to Highland balls, and matching satin slippers, and her dark hair was loose and held back by a wreath of white rosebuds. Though Nurse Boniface and the servants had nagged at her, she had refused to wear a tartan sash or anything tartan at all. "I'm not Scottish," Helen had said, "and it wouldn't be right."

"*You* look absolutely splendid," she said now to Alex, who turned away and told her not to be daft.

But Helen was quite right. Alex didn't care for dressing up, but you can't be a MacBuff of Carra and not know how it is done. The black velvet jacket and the dress kilt had belonged to his father when he was a boy, and the eagle's-head brooch that fastened his plaid was of beaten silver and was five hundred years old.

"Our last night at Green Meadows," said Helen. They were coming back to sleep because the security arrangements were not quite complete at the castle and then, tomorrow, they would move in properly. *And a week after that, Alex is leaving,* thought Helen, her stomach crunching up in a most disagreeable way.

But it was silly to think of that, and ungrateful, when there was so much to be thankful for. Silly, too, to wish she could dance like other girls. She knew all the dances: The Gay Gordons, The Dashing White Sergeant, but what was the use of that?

For a moment, Helen's old sadness came flooding back. It was going to be hard standing by the wall and watching Lillianne, with her dimples and her ringlets, swirling around the room to all those rousing tunes. Very hard.

"Time to go!" said Mr. Hopgood, coming into the room. And then: "My word, what a handsome couple!"

Then he put Helen's wrap around her shoulders and they left for the ball.

18

I T WAS THE ghosts' last night in the cinema. They had meant to glide away at midnight, but when they discovered that there was to be an all-night showing of Scottish films, they decided to stay until morning. *Raiders of the Glen* began at eleven o'clock, but before that they were going to say good-bye to Carra.

Just before they were due to leave, Flossie gave a little shriek and pounced on something that had been hidden under one of the seats. Then she picked up her treasure and snapped it open and snapped it shut. Next, she threw it up in the air, making it loop the loop the way poltergeists do. Her green eyes shone and she giggled happily. But Uncle Louse, leaning forward in his wheelchair, had turned deathly pale, and his head shook on his withered neck.

"Teeth!" he murmured hungrily. "Teeth!"

It was true. What Flossie had found was a perfectly good set of false teeth. How anyone could leave them in a cinema was hard to understand, but people did sometimes take their snappers out when they wanted to be comfortable.

"Flossie, bring them here," ordered Miss Spinks.

But Flossie was too pleased with her new toy to part with it at once. She sent the teeth flying up to the balcony, she made them clack up and down in midair and do somersaults. But at last she came over to Uncle Louse and laid them in his lap.

The next moments were among the most exciting that the ghosts could remember. Uncle Louse picked up the teeth with a shaking hand, and slowly—very slowly—put them in his mouth.

They fitted. Not perfectly, but not badly, either. There is always some looseness with new teeth.

"Oh, I wouldn't have believed it," he murmured, and there were tears in his eyes. "It's a miracle, that's what it is." He snapped the dentures shut, ground them together, made chomping noises. "I'm myself again now; you'll see!"

The old vampire was so happy that Krok decided not to worry about whether the teeth would learn to vanish when Uncle Louse did. After all, out on the prairie these things probably didn't matter as much as all that.

None of them guessed how soon Uncle Louse's new-found teeth would be brought into use—and in a most unexpected and rather dreadful way!

Inside the castle, Alex stood beside Mr. Hopgood and Helen, welcoming the guests, and as they passed him, the people of Granite Falls pressed Alex's hand and said how proud they were to meet a real Scottish laird and what an honor he was doing to their city.

But it was Helen who surprised the guests. Most of them hadn't seen her since she'd had polio and they'd heard how delicate she was, that she could hardly walk, that it wasn't even certain that she was going to live till she was grown up. And what they saw was a bright-faced girl, flushed and pretty, a source of pride to any father.

After they had been welcomed, the guests were given delicious things to eat and drink. Then, punctually at ten o'clock, the band marched into the hall; the first rousing notes of The Gay Gordons rang out . . .

And everybody looked at Alex!

A Highland ball has to be started by the laird, who chooses one girl to go forward onto the floor, and then all the other couples join in and the dancing begins.

Who would Alex choose to open this most important ball? The mayor's wife? Or the lady senator who had flown in specially from Washington and was already slipping off her shawl?

Helen didn't wonder; she knew. He would ask Lillianne, who was cute and had won prizes for ballet and tap. Lillianne had come to tea sometimes and said things like: "Oh, you poor thing, it must be *awful* being lame!"

She bit her lip and stared down at the floor so as not to see Lillianne smirk and toss her curls with their dozens of tartan ribbons when Alex led her out.

"Come on!"

Alex had never thought about anything so obvious as who he would open the ball with. Now he stood in front of Helen and, feeling that perhaps he'd been a bit rude, he grinned and said, "I mean, will you do me the honor of this dance?"

Helen flushed and shook her head. Then she whispered, "I can't, Alex; you know I can't."

"Look, the steps are easy. Just watch me, I'll push you around."

"It isn't that. I know the steps. It's my—"

"Oh, for Pete's *sake,* not that stuff again." Taking no notice of the people watching, he pulled Helen out onto the floor. "If you can ride and swim, you can dance. Or do you suppose I'm going to ask that poisonous-looking kid over there all done up in tartan ribbons like a box of shortbread?"

Then Helen smiled. She forgot her long years of being ill and different from other children. She forgot her fears and her father, half rising from his chair to try and stop her.

She curtsied. Alex bowed. The other couples took their places. And as skillfully and happily as anyone in the room, Helen Hopgood began to dance!

As the ghosts flew out of the cinema, they could see the line for *Raiders of the Glen* shuffling into the building, and everybody in it was gazing up at the floodlit castle.

For all the watchers that night, Carra was a sight to remember, but for the ghosts who had lived there all their haunting lives, it was almost more than they could bear.

"Oh, how beautiful it looks!" cried Miss Spinks—and the tears ran down her cheeks, making them even wetter than before.

"Ah, listen to the pipers!" said Uncle Louse. "There's no music like it in the world."

"Look, there's that set of armor I jumped out of to try and frighten the window cleaner to death in 1753," said Krok. They were level with the top story of the West Tower now and could see into the rooms quite clearly.

"And the chimney corner where I used to sit with Henny . . ." (Uncle Louse's teeth had *not* vanished when he did, but down below the people were far too busy to notice.)

"Oh, the pain of leaving! Oh, the sorrow and sadness!" Miss Spinks's hair came down, and she beat her feet together. "I must go and drown myself—I must drown myself *completely* in the well."

Fortunately, there were so many people milling around the courtyard that Miss Spinks couldn't get *at* the well. All the same, it was agony just hanging there, unwanted and shut out, and when the poltergeist pressed her little face against the window and said, "I—Flossie wants to go *home!*" even Krok felt a lump come to his throat.

"We'll just go down and have a look at the banqueting hall," he said, "and then we'll go. There's no point in making ourselves wretched. Here, Cyril, come to heel!"

The ghosts drifted down until they were level with the great windows. There was a lull now in the dancing; some of the guests had gone off for more refreshments, others had gone down to the cloakrooms to freshen themselves up.

"If only the boy could have seen the place like this," said Uncle Louse as they gazed hungrily at the familiar hall, the vaulted beams with their banners, the stone arches decked with greenery.

"Good-bye forever, dear, dear Carra," said Miss Spinks, kissing the window ledge with sad, wet lips.

"Come!" Krok took hold of her hair, for the madness glittered badly in her eyes.

The others turned to follow him—all except Cyril. The hellhound seemed to have gone off his head. His eyes bulged; he sniffed; he slobbered. He turned around and around in circles; he reared up and scratched the window with his little paws. Any minute now he would become visible, and what then?

"Cyril! Here!"

The dog took not the slightest notice. His tail whirred like a propeller, and now he let out a series of high, shrill, desperately excited yaps.

"Quiet!" Krok looked anxiously down to where two police officers stood, protecting the entrance to the castle.

But Miss Spinks, who had drifted back to help calm Cyril, now gave a shriek and her hand flew to her mouth. "A wraith!" she cried. "A spirit has entered the hall. It is the spirit of dear, dear Alex! Though his body is far away, he appears before us."

The other ghosts crowded around the window. "That's no spirit," said Uncle Louse hoarsely. "That's the boy himself!"

Cyril gave another high, excited volley of yaps.

And in the hall, Alex looked up at the window. Anyone else would have seen only the night sky and the scudding clouds—but Alex saw much more than that.

He gave a little cry and moved forward—and as he came toward them, the ghosts thought they had never seen anyone look so happy as he looked then.

"I don't believe it! I just don't believe it! How did you *get* here? Oh, ghosts, I am so *glad* to be with you again."

Alex had excused himself to Mr. Hopgood and Helen and hurried out, and now they were all in the parking lot of the Rex Cinema, crouched between a Cadillac and a Ford.

There was so much to tell that they scarcely knew where to begin. Alex heard about the unkindness of the Dunloon ghosts and the crossing in the *Queen Anne,* and they realized that he must have flown over the ship on the way to Texas.

"And I—Flossie saw the Big Blob," said the poltergeist for the third time, tugging at Alex's sleeve.

Strangest of all was that they had been so close to one another for three months and never known.

"Anyway, one thing is certain," said Alex when they had told one another everything, "and that is that we're not going to be separated, ever again. I'm staying here another fortnight, and when I go home you're coming with me. Maybe you could become school ghosts during the term, and in the holidays we'll all be together at Sethsay. Even roughing it a bit would be better than being parted."

The ghosts were overjoyed. To think they were going to be with their own dear laird again and in their own country! No spooks called Big Knucklebone, no loneliness, no exile. . . .

"Can you manage in the cinema until then?" asked Alex. "I *know* Helen wouldn't be frightened of you, but Mr. Hopgood just won't see sense about that, and it's not worth making a fuss now."

"Of course we can," said Krok. "It's not such a bad place, and perhaps our friend in the mine may become glorious before we leave."

"That would be great," said Alex, who'd been very interested in the Hand's story. "They're really something, those Hands of Glory. I've read about them."

Miss Spinks then inquired about Helen Hopgood. "Was she the . . . well-covered one with the tartan ribbons or the little thin one in the white dress?"

"Definitely the one in the white dress," said Alex, and the ghosts were very relieved. They had liked the look of Helen as much as they had *not* liked the look of the other girl.

But Flossie was feeling neglected. She was obviously the most important person there and Alex had not heard nearly all her adventures.

"I—Flossie did see a lady with coming-off bosoms," she said, putting a hand on Alex's arm.

"Quiet, Flossie! How can you start that rude talk again when dear Alex is restored to us?" said Miss Spinks.

The poltergeist scowled. "I—Flossie did *so* see her. First she was a lady on the boat and played nasty music, and then she was a man with hairy knees and dug holes in the ground. Here he did, right in the castle."

"Flossie, if you don't stop—"

But the Viking was frowning. "Wait! I've just remembered something. It was from the Zugorsky Trio that I heard that Carra was to be rebuilt. They were standing by the cabin window...." Krok rubbed his forehead, trying to recall what he had heard. "Madame Zugorsky was very large with broad shoulders ... perhaps the child is right; she could have been a man. They spoke about something being a breeze once the Hopgoods had moved. I didn't take much notice at the time, but now I think of it, they sounded as though they were up to no good. There was a woman with long black hair—though I suppose it might have been a wig. She had a gold locket she kept pawing...."

"Could they be planning to steal something from the castle?" suggested Uncle Louse. "Mr. Hopgood's paintings ... or his money?"

"I don't know." Alex's voice was very low. "Look, I must get back now—I'll come and find you in the cinema tomorrow and then we'll make plans."

They said good-bye and Alex crossed the parking lot, showed his pass to the policeman at the gates, and entered the castle. He had been walking very fast, but now he began to run. If thieves were after Mr. Hopgood's paintings or his money, he should be warned. If that was what they were after . . . *If* . . .

I'm being ridiculous, thought Alex. *In a minute I'll see Helen with her wreath a bit askew from dancing so hard.*

He entered the ballroom, furious with himself because of the way his heart was thumping—and at once Mr. Hopgood hurried over.

"Ah, there you are, Alex," he said. "But where's Helen? Surely she's with you?"

IT WAS DARK. Pitch-dark and terribly cold. There was a black vault above her from which something icy dripped onto a place just behind her head. Her hands were bound and her wrists were sore and chafed. She was still wearing her white dress, but she'd been roughly bundled into some sort of blanket. Even so, the chill seemed to strike right into her bones.

Where can I be? thought Helen. *What has happened?* She tried to think back. When she'd finished dancing with Alex, she'd gone down to the cloakroom to tidy her hair . . . only something was wrong with the light switch; it wouldn't go on. Then someone had come forward . . . a woman in a dark coat. She'd thought the woman was trying to help her, but almost at once she'd felt a jab in her arm. And after that, nothing. . . . She could remember nothing.

Helen tried to move, but the ropes that bound her only bit harder into her wrists. She seemed to be in a kind of cave, a recess in the side of a tunnel hollowed out of bare rock. A railway tunnel? As her eyes became more used to the dark, she could make out some rails, but they were too small for a proper train.

Oh, God, thought Helen, *what has happened? Who wants to harm me? Am I to be killed?*

She tried to call out, but the drug she'd been given was still making her drowsy, and only a faint mewing sound, like that of a wounded bird, came from her lips. Even so, it brought someone. Footsteps could be heard coming along the tunnel, and a flashlight was flashed cruelly into her eyes.

"You're awake, are you?"

Helen gasped. The face that bent over her was distorted by a stocking mask, but the outline of the gun pressed into her ribs was clear enough.

"Where am I?" Helen tried very hard to hold her voice steady, but it wavered pitifully.

"Never mind where you are," blustered Ratty. "You'll stay here until your father's paid five million dollars—and you'd better not move or make a fuss, or it'll be the worse for you."

"Oh, not *seriously* the worse." Helen had not heard the second person approach—a woman whose face, too, was blurred by a mask, but whose oily voice seemed familiar. "Perhaps we might remove one ear and send it to your father. Not *both* ears, just one." She put down her lamp and took out a pearl-handled knife, which she moved up and down, getting closer and closer to Helen's cheek. "Pretty, isn't it?" purred Adolfa. "The pearls are real—and it's *so* sharp. There's no messy *sawing* with a knife like that. But you're going to be good, I'm sure. All little girls are fond of their ears; it's only natural."

She moved away down the tunnel and the man followed. Left alone in the dark, Helen began to feel a fear so terrible that she thought it would kill her. *I can't bear it,* she thought; *I can't, I can't.*

Only I must bear it, I must. I must keep absolutely calm and quiet and then perhaps there will be something I can do. I must think about nice things. Not about my father; he'll be so wretched. . . . Not about my mother, either—I don't know if people can really look down from heaven, but I expect it's not as simple as that.

But Alex . . . yes, I can think about Alex. . . . And Patagonia . . . I'll think about the boat we're going to go in through the fjords . . . a blue boat with a red sail, but not only a sail, of course—that would be silly. We must have an outboard motor as well. I'll think about the camp we're going to make at the foot of the mountains and the fish we're going to grill over the fire.

People who are going to Patagonia don't scream because they're lying bound in a tunnel. Nothing has happened yet . . . my wrists don't really hurt. Not really. . . .

I can think about the ponies we're going to ride up into the forest. They'll be shaggy and strong and a bit wild . . . or maybe they'll be mules with twitchy ears. There'll be wild deer and lots of butterflies . . . and then we'll come to the cave where they found the sloth hairs in 1902. . . .

A cave in Patagonia would be as dark as this, and as cold. The weather's very bad in Patagonia. Alex would say it was good practice being imprisoned here like this. That's what I must think about, what good practice this is.

From far down the tunnel there came the sound of the dreadful woman's sudden laughter.

Helen began to shiver uncontrollably, and tears welled up under her eyelids.

"I *won't* cry," she said to herself, bringing her teeth down hard on her lower lip. "But, oh, *please,* God, don't let them cut off my ear!"

They had searched the castle from top to bottom—the armory, the gallery, the dungeons, the battlements—calling and calling. The guests had joined in, shouting "Coo-ee!" or "Helen, where are you?"—at first quite light-heartedly, then getting more and more worried and desperate. The pipers in their kilts had joined in the search, and the waiters and the cloakroom attendants, and of course the grim-faced security men.

After an hour, no one pretended anymore. Helen Hopgood had vanished.

Now Mr. Hopgood lay on a couch in the library surrounded by police officers. His face was gray and covered in a film of sweat. A doctor had been called, but Mr. Hopgood wouldn't take any pills to make him calmer or even let the doctor feel his pulse.

"Find her. . . . For God's sake, find her," was all he could say.

"We'll find her, sir," said the young lieutenant. "We've got thirty men now searching every stick and stone, and a pack of tracker dogs. We'll find her for sure."

But he was not as hopeful as he pretended. That the Hopgood girl could be snatched from under the very noses of the security men who thronged the castle meant that the gang who'd done the job was very smart indeed.

The waiting was terrible. Minute by minute, the wretched night crawled past. The guests had left; the rooms were deserted. In the courtyard only the police with their vans and searchlights and walkie-talkies remained.

If only I hadn't left Helen when I saw the ghosts, thought Alex, sitting hunched up in the window seat. *If only I'd taken her with me. It's all my fault.*

He looked down to see a police car coming over the drawbridge, and a few moments later, two detectives came hurrying in.

"There's news, sir! We've found these in the woods behind the Three Star Ranch. Could you identify them as belonging to your daughter?"

Mr. Hopgood looked up, gasped, and clutched his heart—and it was Alex who answered.

"Yes, those are Helen's."

But he, too, had to turn away and swallow the lump that had come up in his throat. Helen's wreath of rosebuds had been trampled in the dust; only a few faded flowers were left, and the sash from her dress had been savagely torn.

"The wreath was quite close to the road, and the sash was half a mile away toward San Fernando. There's no doubt she's being held up in the hills somewhere."

"We'll have the helicopters out as soon as it's light, and the dogs are there already, along with every man we've got," said the second detective. "But we were wondering if you felt like coming along with us, sir? You might recognize something else your daughter wore. A pin or a brooch?"

Mr. Hopgood struggled to his feet. "Yes . . . yes . . . of course I'll come."

The officer turned to Alex. "What about you?"

Alex shook his head. "I'll stay."

Only why did I say that? he asked himself, left alone in the library. *What's the point of staying here when it's clear that Helen's miles away? And why do I keep on thinking about what Flossie said: "First she was a lady . . . and then he was a man and dug holes in the castle."*

What holes? The holes for the dungeons? But the dungeons led nowhere—it wasn't as though Carra had a secret passage. And Helen's wreath had been found behind the Three Star Ranch.

Yet even as he was thinking this, Alex found himself on the stone staircase that led underground.

Back in Scotland there would have been cheerful rats to squeak and scamper across his shoes, but Mr. Hopgood had drawn the line at rats, and it was as quiet as the grave.

How often he'd played down here with the ghosts, swinging on the iron hoops that the prisoners had been chained to, or pretending to hide in the old broom cupboard that the wife of the eighth MacBuff had built when the dungeons were no longer used to starve prisoners to death, but were just used to store things. It had been splendid for playing sardines, that cupboard; it was big enough for him to lie down, and then all the ghosts would come one by one. Except that Flossie always squeaked and gave the game away.

He wandered over and opened it. In Carra there'd been nothing much in it except old buckets and brushes and coils of rope, but now there were overalls hanging on hooks at the back and tins of paint and a vacuum. No one had vacuumed at Carra—the rats wouldn't have stood for it.

Alex stepped into the cupboard, remembering the familiar smell of mildew and dust.

Yes, it was all just as it was . . . except that there was a draft around his ankles, which was odd because the walls there were three feet thick—and the draft came from the *back*. From the solid back wall of the cupboard. . . .

Alex's heart began to pound. He felt with his hands along the wood.

Nothing. It was just an old slab of wood, and now he had a splinter as well. He was about to turn away when his fingers came up against something concealed behind one of the overalls. A handle . . .

Alex pulled . . . pulled again . . . and stumbled backward as the wall of the cupboard opened like a door.

Facing him was a narrow, freshly dug tunnel that bent almost at once to the left.

Forgetting common sense, forgetting everything except that he might find Helen, Alex went forward into the dark.

...

The ghosts in the cinema were having a splendid time. *Raiders of the Glen* was about two rival clansmen who murdered each other in all sorts of interesting ways— sometimes cutting each other down with swords, sometimes leaping at each other from trees and fastening their legs around each other's throats, and sometimes boring holes in each other's boats so that they drowned. And *The Monster of the Loch,* which came next, was even better.

Only the day before, the film would have made them dreadfully homesick, but now, knowing that they were going back to Scotland with their dear laird, they were pleased with everything and didn't even mind when the hero and heroine kissed each other for far too long.

Not only were the films good, but the cinema looked really festive! The manager had engaged extra ushers in frilly tartan dresses to serve the audience with ice cream in the MacBuff colors and chocolate haggises and bagpipes made of licorice, and there wasn't a spare seat in the house.

After the third film ended at dawn, there was a gap while the cinema was cleaned and the ghosts had a little nap. Soon, though, the place started filling up again, because the manager had arranged to go on showing Scottish films all that day and the next. But the people who filed in for the morning show had grave faces and spoke to one another in low voices, for by now it was known that Helen Hopgood had been kidnapped and that though the police had been searching all through the night, there was no sign of her. It was known, too, that when Mr. Hopgood had heard that the Scottish boy had vanished also, he'd collapsed.

"They fear for his health, poor soul," said one lady as she bought a jawbreaker stamped with a picture of Carra Castle for her son.

But the ghosts, hanging cheerfully in the beam from the projection box, knew none of this. Any minute now, Alex would come and find them, and as the curtains parted for *Orphan of the Isles,* they settled down to enjoy themselves.

20

I'M SORRY, HELEN. I was such an idiot."

"You weren't. You were splendid. Only I don't want anything to happen to you. Your father isn't a millionaire."

"Nothing's going to happen to either of us," said Alex. "Your father'll pay the ransom and they'll let you go and that'll be that."

"I won't go unless they let you go, too."

"Don't be silly."

He lay beside Helen, bound hand and foot, in a dark alcove off the central chamber of the mine. Though he spoke bravely, Alex felt anything but brave. He'd crawled through the tunnel right into an ambush. What's more, he'd recognized the masked woman who'd reared up in front of him, gloatingly pushing her knife into his ribs. As she bent toward him, her coat had opened a little and her locket had swung forward, catching the light. He knew she was Adolfa Batters—and knew, too, that she was the woman that Krok had seen on the boat.

And Adolfa knew that he knew. Which meant that he was going to be killed.

There seemed no way to bear the thought. He didn't feel like a MacBuff of Carra going to a noble death; he felt like a rat in the jaws of a dog, shaken and gripped by terror.

"It would have been . . . nice . . . to go to Patagonia, wouldn't it?" The cold and the drugs she had been given were making Helen dangerously drowsy. That was how people perished in the snow. They just went to sleep and drifted away. Maybe if he couldn't save himself, he could save Helen.

"Don't talk like that. We will go. We'll do everything we said we would."

"And . . . will we find him?"

"The giant sloth? Of *course* we'll find him. Only not in a cave. We'll be riding through the forest and the ponies will stop and make that whickering noise and not want to go any farther. So we'll get off and go on foot, very quietly—and then we'll see something . . . a shape . . . only we won't believe it at first."

"Because it'll be so big?"

Alex nodded. "But it'll be him. Not hanging upside down, because the giant ones don't—just lying there like a sleepy old gentleman with his fur blowing a bit in the breeze. And then he'll open his eyes—big, round, golden eyes they'll be. . . ."

"Will he be afraid of us?"

"No. Because we'll be the first humans he's ever seen." Alex was silent for a moment. "Only I think you were right, Helen. We'll just photograph him and leave him there. Not catch him and truss him up and take him back to a zoo."

In the central chamber of the mine, lit by two hurricane lamps, Adolfa rose from her deck chair and put down her knitting.

"Right; I'm off to see if the ransom demand's through. By the time I'm back, the boy's to be at the bottom of the pool. No point in wasting a bullet."

She pointed to the third of the tunnels—the one that led neither to the castle nor the cinema, but to the collapsed shaft and the black, fathomless pool of floodwater that had collected there.

"Can't I wait until Oscar comes back?" asked Ratty. "He's more used to all that."

"Now look, Ratty, I don't want to get cross with you," said Adolfa softly, running her knife gently up and down Ratty's cheek. "Even your funny little biceps should be equal to pushing a child that's bound hand and foot to the edge of a pool and shoving him in. If you're too feeble to lift him, drag him. If you have to cut his throat first, then do it, but I want as little mess as possible."

She took off her coat, felt for the zipper hidden in the ruffle of her long tartan dress, and unzipped it. Then she stepped out of the lower part of her skirt and picked up her flashlight. Dressed like that, she looked exactly like all the other ushers in the Rex Cinema.

"And the girl?"

"She can stay where she is for now. If there's any fuss about the money, we may still have to send her father a reminder—a finger or an ear."

Adolfa scowled. She'd meant to leave Helen in the mine for the police to find—or not—once they were on their way home as the Zugorsky Trio. But the boy had messed everything up. Helen, too, now knew more than was safe.

Ratty, left alone, felt gloomy. It wasn't nice in the mine. Oscar was still out in a fast car, hoodwinking the police, while he was here doing boring things. Nasty things, too—dragging the boy to the pool, where he'd plop and scream and bob up again, maybe.

He put his gun down on Adolfa's chair and buckled

on his knife. It was all so unfair, thought Ratty. Adolfa's knife was nicer than his and Oscar's muscles were bigger than his. Oscar was stupid, but his biceps were like grapefruits and his thighs were like the trunks of trees.

All the same, I'll show them, thought Ratty, picking up a lamp and pulling off his face mask. Since both kids were for the high jump, there was no point in getting itchy. *When I've done Mr. Guggenfelder's exercises a bit longer, my biceps'll be like melons and I'll bulge all over. And they'd better not push me around then!*

The children were lying where he'd left them, side by side under the blanket. The girl seemed to be asleep, but the boy was wide-awake.

Perhaps I'll limber up a bit, Ratty decided. You had to be in the mood to cut people's throats and drown them. He slapped his skinny shoulders with his arms, then squatted down on his haunches, stuck out a leg, and rolled his head around and around on his scraggy neck.

"Isn't that one of Mr. Guggenfelder's strengthening exercises?" asked Alex. The waiter's son in Torquay had been very keen on bodybuilding.

"Yes, it is." Ratty straightened himself, flexed one arm, and took the pose that the champion wrestler held on the cover of his book.

"You *are* strong," said Alex admiringly, looking at the

pinhead-sized lump that had come up under Ratty's jersey. "Can you do the one where you hook one leg behind the other one and then unroll your back? The spine strengthener?"

" 'Course I can."

Standing on one leg, the little man wobbled badly, but the knife stayed firmly in its sheath.

"That's not bad," said Alex. "But when I saw Mr. Guggenfelder on TV, he had his arms crossed behind his back as well. He said that really pumped the muscles. You could almost *hear* them growing!"

Ratty grunted, and twisted his arms behind him. He writhed; he wriggled—but the knife was still in place.

"There!" he gasped. Then he untangled himself and moved closer to Alex. Better get on with the job. . . .

"That was fantastic!" said Alex quickly. "Terrific! I'd almost think you could do the Guggenfelder reefer."

"Almost? What d'yer mean, *almost*? 'Course I can do it."

Ratty whipped the blanket off Alex and sat down on it. He put his right hand under his left armpit and his left hand under his right armpit. Then he drew up his knees, jammed his greasy head between them, and tried to lift his buttocks off the ground.

"That's the *single* reefer," said Alex contemptuously. "I mean the *double* reefer—the one where you put your ankles behind your neck. Only about three people in the world can do that."

Ratty gritted his teeth. He'd never heard of the Guggenfelder double reefer, but he wasn't going to admit it.

He lifted his left leg. He pulled at it, he tugged at it—he fell over. Then he straightened himself, took hold of the right leg, managed to hook it behind his head, picked up the left leg again . . .

And the knife fell to the ground.

"You've almost done it." *(Oh, please, God, don't let him notice!)* "But you have to get your ankles so far around that your toes almost touch your ears—and *then* your hands go under your armpits."

And Alex rolled over as if to show Ratty. He was on the edge of the blanket!

Ratty yanked at his ankles; he crossed his hands and stuck them under his arms. . . . And then he saw the knife! Frantically, he tried to free his right arm, but as he pulled, the muscles only seemed to tighten. The left arm, then. . . . Only which was his left and which was his right? His limbs were completely muddled up.

"You have to squeeze your armpits together. That's how you get free," said Alex—and rolled over once again.

Ratty squeezed. "Ow! I've got cramp! I'm stuck! I'm knotted!"

Alex was on top of the knife. He was levering it against the rope that bound his wrists.

The little crook was still tied up in a welter of arms and legs, squealing with rage and pain, as Alex freed Helen, and the children ran away down the tunnel and out of sight.

21

THIS FILM'S KIND of slow, Ma," said a boy called Joe Peters, sitting between his mother and his sister in the front row of the Rex Cinema. "Can I have another chocolate haggis?"

Orphan of the Isles was a bit slow. The orphan was a girl called Fiona who'd been imprisoned by her wicked stepfather in the cellar of his castle because she'd helped Bonnie Prince Charlie find a horse. The stepfather was on the side of the English, who were against the noble prince, and he was treating Fiona very badly, keeping her in her nightdress and not giving her enough to eat. Fiona had a friend, a true Scottish boy called Hamish, who was a cowherd (though of noble blood) and wandered about tending his cattle in full Highland dress, which is unusual, but it was that kind of film. Hamish had got hold of a file and was trying to free Fiona, but he was taking his time.

"Why doesn't he get on and saw through the bars?" Joe wanted to know.

The cinema was packed, the tartan ushers were everywhere, and the sweets were fine, but it was no good pretending that *Orphan of the Isles* was coming up to scratch. You can always tell whether a film is good by how full the lavatories are, and the lavatories that morning were crammed with children who wanted a change from sitting still.

Then, suddenly, the most amazing thing happened. The film turned into a proper 3-D spectacle! The hero and heroine came right out of the film and into the cinema. Up on the screen, Hamish and Fiona had escaped and were hiding from the wicked stepfather in a churchyard—and now both of them had appeared from under the stage and were running up the aisle!

"Hey, look, it's the feelies!" yelled Joe.

And, really, it was extraordinary! The girl in the white nightdress and the boy in the kilt were exactly like the ones on the screen—and the way they looked over their shoulders to see if they were being followed was the same. This was the best trick photography they'd ever seen, thought the kids, and they stamped their feet and cheered.

But that wasn't all. Because the wicked stepfather had come out of the same place and started to run after the children. He'd shrunk a bit, but it was him, all right, with his horrible foxy face.

"Boo!" shrieked the children in the audience. "Get away! Leave them alone!"—and Joe's little sister tried to throw her ice cream at the nasty man.

"Hurry, Helen!" Alex, panting, dragged her by the hand. Ratty had a gun, and his mad shrieks as he'd unknotted himself and chased them through the mine made it likely that he might fire even in this crowded place.

They were almost at the top of the aisle, and here now was an usher hurrying toward them. She'd help them! Ratty wouldn't dare to do anything while they were talking to an usher. They were safe at last!

"Please help us," begged Alex, fighting for breath. "We've been held down in the mine and we have to get out to the police."

A flashlight beamed into his eyes. A very strong flashlight; stronger, surely, than the ones that ushers had usually? At the same time, Helen cried out and Alex saw a flash of silver against her cheek.

"Certainly I will help you, my dears," said Adolfa Batters. "Certainly. All you have to do is come with me very quietly to that side exit over there. Very quietly indeed.

I've only made a little gash in your friend's face, but there's more to come, I promise you."

"Oh, no!" It was all Alex could do not to spring at Adolfa's throat.

Adolfa now had nothing to lose. She had to kill the children at once—both of them—and make her escape, leaving Oscar to follow with the money. The side exit led to a deserted alleyway and a patch of waste ground . . . and the Ferrari was parked nearby.

"That's right," whispered Adolfa, her knife still pricking Helen's face. "I thought you'd see it my way. Just keep on walking."

Ratty had recognized Adolfa and stood waiting with his gun. The children in the audience were quiet now, not sure what was happening.

They'd reached the side aisle that led off to the exit. Only a few more steps and they'd be alone with Adolfa, thought Alex. There'd be no hope for them then.

There was no hope for them now.

Or was there? "Helen, whatever happens now you mustn't be afraid," whispered Alex. Then he threw back his head, and in a voice that rang through the cinema, he called out: "Oh, ghosts of Carra, appear and come to my aid!"

No one in the audience ever forgot what happened next.

On the screen there was still the churchyard where the children had been hiding. But the cinema now seemed to get very cold, and a dark mist swirled around the beam of light from the projection box.

And then the most extraordinary things appeared on the screen! From behind one of the tombstones there floated a long gray lady with trailing hair and webbed feet. A stone coffin changed into a creaking chair with wheels, and sitting in it was a dreadful specter with a withered neck. The weathervane on top of the church turned into a pair of hairy feet and then into a mighty warrior who swung his battle-ax and shouted, "Death to the enemies of the MacBuffs!"

And then the ghosts swooshed out of the screen and into the cinema itself!

The children went wild. These were the best special effects they'd ever seen. It was fantastic; it was uncanny; it was unbelievable!

"It's a spook film! It's spooks to the rescue," they yelled—and Joe Peters's little sister said, "I want the ghost with ducky feet," and fell off her seat.

It was Cyril who reached Adolfa first, rearing up in front of her, fully visible and as horrible as he'd ever been in Hades, and Adolfa, seeing his fiery muzzle and slavering jaws, staggered backward—and dropped her knife.

And Alex grabbed Helen's hand and ran.

Too late. Ratty was at the exit before them.

"Stop or I'll shoot," he hissed. And then, "*Eeek!* Go away! Shoo!"

Miss Spinks was not often cross, but she was cross now. Poor dear Alex being chased by these vulgar people . . . She lay back in midair, hitched up her skirts, and came at Ratty with her feet, banging him like a battering ram about the face. At the same time Uncle Louse, above her, positioned his chair.

"You can't scare me," gabbled Ratty. "You're just trick photography." But the webbed feet were soaking wet and dreadful, and the teeth snapping above him looked hideously real. Ratty shivered and shook and tried to beat the things off with his free hand, but he still held his gun—and it pointed at Alex.

There was no way past. Back, then. . . . If they could get across to the far side of the cinema, they could make their way around to the main doors and out into the street.

"Oh, no, you don't!"

Adolfa barred the way. Her flashlight shone cruelly into their eyes; her bony arm gripped Helen's and twisted it—and she had found her knife.

Above Adolfa, somebody giggled. Then an entire tray of sweets rose up in the air, flew across the cinema—and turned upside down.

"Gloop! Garrugle! Splish!"

Adolfa's face was covered in gunge from the chocolate haggises; jawbreakers rained down on her head—and as she groped and spluttered and the children cheered, the tray itself came down and hit her on the chest.

"We'll make it now, Helen."

Spent as she was, blood trickling from the cut behind her ear, Helen managed to run with Alex. They were almost at the top of the aisle, almost in the safety of the street.

No! Ratty might be terrified of the trick photography, but he was more terrified still of Adolfa and, racing up the side gangway, he reached the doors before them.

"Get them!" yelled Adolfa, spitting out a licorice bagpipe. "Get them or I'll have your guts for garters!"

"It's no use," sobbed Helen. "We'll never get out."

Ratty leveled his gun. But now the giggling noise could be heard again and then another sound. *Twang!* Something had snapped. The next moment Ratty's trousers, with their broken suspenders, came down and fell across his feet.

"He's in his underpants; he's in his underpants," screeched the children in the audience, falling about.

Flossie had done one of her best tricks. What's more, she'd given Uncle Louse the help he needed. He'd missed once, but he wasn't going to miss again. Carefully he took aim . . . opened his mouth . . . charged.

It was the end of Ratty. He made a noise like a hundred pigs in a slaughterhouse and dropped on his hands and knees. "I'm done for, I'm bit, I've got rabies," he babbled. "I'm frothing, I'm finished!" And he crawled along the aisle, barking like a dog.

"I'll say you're finished," said Adolfa. She leaped over him, seized his gun, and whacked him hard on the side of the head.

"I'm bit; I'm bit in the throat!" screamed Ratty—and Adolfa bopped him once more and straightened herself, ready to finish off Alex and Helen.

Only where were they?

"They've gone that way! They've gone past you— they're out into the street," yelled the children gleefully.

"No, they haven't!" shouted one truly horrible little boy (whom the others thumped afterward in the parking lot). "They've gone back where they came from!"

Adolfa looked down the aisle and saw a last glimmer of white as Helen vanished under the stage. That they should double back into the mine was the last thing she'd expected. If they managed to get through into the castle, everything was lost.

With a whoop of rage, she rushed down toward the screen—and the ghosts of Carra followed.

• • •

In the mine, Adolfa went berserk. Realizing that the creatures that were chasing her were not part of the film, but proper ghosts, unhinged her completely. As she ran she shrieked, and as she shrieked she fired her pistol.

The first three shots ricocheted harmlessly off the walls of the tunnel, but the third whizzed past Helen's shoulder.

"Down, Helen—she's really mad now."

Alex kicked over a lamp, and they ducked behind one of the trolleys.

"I see you, I see you," screamed Adolfa, weaving about in the dark.

"We're here!" shouted Alex, bobbing up briefly—and Adolfa fired two more shots in his direction—and missed.

That was five bullets she'd used. Only one more.

But Adolfa was coming to her senses. She was moving closer, peering, holding her fire.

"*Eeeek!*" The last bullet went hopelessly wide as Adolfa stepped on something unspeakable—something white and dismembered and loathsome, which scuttled away like a spider.

And Alex leaped to his feet and ran.

"No, Alex. No!" Helen's desperate shout came too late.

Barring the entrance to the castle tunnel stood a huge hulk of a man who reached out a gorilla arm for Alex.

"Kill him, kill him!" screamed Adolfa, searching about for Helen. "Take no notice of the disgusting spooks."

But Alex had wriggled free . . . he was running back across the central chamber toward the collapsed mine shaft and the bottomless pool.

And Oscar followed!

Near the edge of the water Alex pressed himself against the wall, and Oscar, who'd rushed past him, turned with his back to the pool—and gasped!

A warrior stood before him, armed to the teeth. A fine-honed ax gleamed in one hand, a sword with a jeweled hilt in the other, and his face and beard shone with a spectral light.

"Your time has come, cur!" pronounced Krok Full-belly. "No man harms the laird of Carra and lives."

"You . . . can't hurt me . . . you're just a sp-spook," gabbled Oscar. But he took a step backward, for the apparition was truly dreadful.

"Make your peace with your gods, hog," said the Viking, raising his ax.

"No, no . . . go away . . . you're not real." But Oscar had fallen on his knees and was gibbering with fear.

Krok kicked him contemptuously. "Rise, worm, and die like a man."

Oscar scrambled to his feet and took another step backward.

"Die!" thundered Krok, and brought down his ax.

Oscar stepped back again.

"Die!" repeated the Viking, and swept his sword through Oscar's neck.

The Hulk stepped back once more. Only this time there was no ground beneath his feet. His arms went out, his legs flew upward—and vanished. There was an unearthly scream . . . and a long time afterward, a splash.

The bottomless pool had claimed Oscar. The Hulk was gone.

But there was no time to rejoice. "Hurry, oh, hurry," begged Alex. "That awful woman has found Helen, I'm sure."

Alex was right. Adolfa was bending over Helen and, as the ghosts surged forward, she greeted them with a mad torrent of words.

"Stand still, you horrible spooks and creepy crawlies! That's what the world has come to . . . vegetarian scum . . . pacifist pigs . . . disgusting dogs fouling the pavements! That's the filth that CREEP is fighting. One step closer and the knife goes through her heart."

"Stop!" Alex commanded his ghosts. "We can't take any chances with Helen."

"Anarchist filth! Unclean monsters—get out, get away! The girl is mine! If you take one step closer, I'll stick her like a pig; I'll hook her; I'll flay her; I'll boil her," shrieked Adolfa, and moved the knife against Helen's ribs.

Helen lay quite still with her eyes closed. It was Alex who cried out.

"I'm going to kill her," gloated Adolfa. "You've spoiled everything, so I'm going to kill her very slowly in front of you, and you can't stop me because you're contaminated spooks, you're worse than university professors, you're yucky filth, you're—"

Then something quite extraordinary happened. Adolfa turned her head to one side, staring at a ledge in the rock. Her mouth fell open and her lower jaw hung there, stuck. The knife clattered from her hand and her arm became entirely rigid. Her neck would not turn nor her back bend. She could neither move nor speak.

At first no one could understand what had happened. Then they saw a glow as blue and bright as sapphires— and in the middle of it, the Hand with his fingers in the STOP position.

The sound of gunfire had woken the Hand from his faint, and being stepped on by the vile Adolfa had shocked him into action. Now, in this hour of need, his wish had been granted. He had become a Hand of Glory—and Adolfa Batters, the great-great-granddaughter of Erik Erikson, was locked and turned to stone.

Alex bent down to help Helen to her feet. The kidnapping was over.

ADOLFA HAD TO BE carried out of the mine; she was as stiff as a board and her eyes were fixed like a zombie's. On the other hand, Ratty had to be shoved into the van by two detectives and a dog handler, and all the way to the police station he writhed and foamed at the mouth and said he had rabies. As for Oscar's body, it still lay at the bottom of the mine shaft. Getting him out of the pool was a job for later.

Now Helen and Alex sat in the banqueting hall of the castle, surrounded by reporters with notebooks and recorders and cameras. Mr. Hopgood sat close to Helen, holding her hand. It seemed as though he couldn't believe that the danger was past, but though he looked gray and ill, Helen was bright-eyed and alert and wouldn't let anyone make a fuss. "I'm perfectly all right now," she said. "It's all over and, no, I'm not going to bed."

"Could you just tell us again how you outwitted the crooks single-handed?" said one of the reporters to Alex, and the others thronged around him, eager for his reply.

"No," said Alex. "I could not."

The reporters looked up from their notebooks, surprised.

"I couldn't because I didn't." He looked at Helen, who smiled and gave a little nod. "I could never have got away on my own and nor could Helen." He got to his feet and walked over to the platform where the band had played. "Ladies and gentlemen," said Alex, "meet the people who did rescue us! Meet the ghosts of Carra and their friend, the Severed Hand."

And as the ghosts appeared, and the Hand tiptoed shyly out from behind a screen, pandemonium broke loose!

It was an hour before the reporters could be cleared out, and when they left, it was to splash stories of the rescue throughout America and the world.

But at last the children and Mr. Hopgood were alone with the ghosts.

"You do realize, Daddy," said Helen, "that from now on Carra *has* to be their home. Forever and ever. And honestly," she went on, scratching Cyril's ear, "I don't know how you could think I'd be frightened of them."

Mr. Hopgood nodded. He'd at last learned the truth about his daughter: that she was a brave and healthy girl. But it wasn't just Helen that Mr. Hopgood had learned about in the last dreadful hours; it was himself. What sort of life was it, being a millionaire? No sort of life at all. His stomach was full of acid, he never had a decent night's sleep, and his daughter was in danger from every vile sort of crook.

"I've decided to retire," said Mr. Hopgood. "I'm going to keep enough money for us to live on comfortably and the rest I'm going to give away. And I wondered," he said to Alex, "whether Helen and I—and the ghosts, of course—might spend part of each year with you on that island of yours—Sethsay. I thought I'd give Carra to the people of Granite Falls and just keep a small apartment in one of the towers for us to use in the winter."

There was no need to ask Helen and Alex what they thought of this plan. Helen threw her arms around her father and hugged him, and Alex said he couldn't think of anything nicer if he tried for a hundred years.

As for the ghosts, they were quite beside themselves with joy, and when the Hand asked if he could come, too, and write a book, there was nothing left to wish for.

But happiness is a funny thing. Often when you feel on top of the world, something quite unexpected comes and topples you.

The hall of the castle became extremely cold. Then a black cloud rolled past the windows. Next came the sound of horses' hooves in the air above them. A very large horse, it seemed to be. . . . Cyril whined and tried to crawl under Alex's chair, and everyone looked up at the sky.

An enormous beast—an eight-legged stallion as black as night—had come to rest outside the window. And on the back of the horse was the fattest, largest woman they had ever seen. Her swelling bosom was covered by a steel breastplate; she wore a helmet over her thick, golden pigtails; her thighs, in their leather breeches, spread to cover the saddle. No wonder she rode an eight-legged horse; a four-legged one would have collapsed under her.

The armored lady now heaved herself off the horse, thrust her spear through the window, sending shattered glass in all directions, and waddled into the room. Taking no notice of anyone else, she stopped in front of Krok and poked him in the stomach.

"Kommet nu ut Valhalla. Forrt!" she said in a voice as deep as a prizefighter's.

The Viking's hand flew to his mouth. He alone knew who she was, or why she had come.

The woman was a Valkyrie, one of the warrior maidens who serve the great Viking god, Odin. And she had come to tell Krok that because he had killed Oscar the Hulk, he was free of his curse and could come up to Valhalla and live with the heroes.

"*Smorgasbord! Schweinkoteletten! Bier!*" the Valkyrie went on, licking her lips.

Krok turned around to explain. "She says I must come quickly, Odin is waiting. There's to be hog meat . . . and feasting . . . and merriment all day long."

"Oh, Krok!" Alex tried desperately to be pleased, but he simply couldn't manage it. "Just when we're all together again! But of course it's marvelous for you."

"Aye." Uncle Louse nodded, but he had to turn his chair away. He and Krok had haunted together for three hundred years, and he'd have given even his newfound teeth to have kept the Viking by his side.

Krok turned back to the Valkyrie. "Actually," he said, speaking carefully because it was a struggle to remember the Viking words, "I have sort of got used to being here on earth—and to being under a curse."

The Valkyrie stamped her foot and the walls of the banqueting hall trembled. How dared he talk like that? To go to Valhalla was the greatest honor that ever befell a warrior. Not only did Viking heroes spend all day feasting, but they each had a Valkyrie to look after them, and she was the one who was going to look after him. "I shall pour your wine and cut up your hog chops and clean the wax out of your ears," she said, jabbing him with her spear. "And I have ninety-nine sisters. So no more talking. Come!"

"I shall have to go," said Krok. "I expect I'm going to be very happy . . . later on, when I've gotten used to it." His voice broke, but he managed to pull himself together. "Of course, some people might say that eating all that pork would give you indigestion, and I've heard there's nothing worse for ears than poking about inside them. . . ."

But the Valkyrie now looked as though she might turn nasty, so they all lined up to say good-bye. It was a miserable business. Even Helen, who'd only just met the Viking, found it painful, and Alex felt as though he was losing a father all over again.

Krok had left saying good-bye to Miss Spinks to the last, but when he moved forward to shake hands with her, there was only a damp and mist-filled space.

It was the last straw for the poor Viking. Here he was, going off forever with a hippopotamus-sized woman who stuck spears into him, and Miss Spinks, whom he'd thought of as his special friend, couldn't even be bothered to see him off. As he climbed onto the horse behind the Valkyrie, wondering if her huge behind would push him off the end, Krok Fullbelly felt as hurt and bitter as he'd ever felt in his life.

What had happened to Miss Spinks was this.

When she saw the Valkyrie, the unfortunate governess was quite overcome by jealousy and grief. The warrior

lady seemed to have everything that she herself did not, and the thought of life without Krok Fullbelly was more than she could bear.

So she decided to drown herself thoroughly, this time for good. And the best place for this, she thought, was the pool at the bottom of the mine shaft, which was dark and deep and bottomless, and would put her out of her misery forever. And while Krok galloped off toward Valhalla, Miss Spinks glided through the mine until she came to the ruined shaft and the edge of the pool.

For a moment, she stood looking down at the water. She had drowned herself a thousand times, but this was different—this was forever. Then she gathered up her skirts and leaped!

As soon as she hit the surface, Miss Spinks felt a deep sense of disappointment. She had thought that the pool would be bottomless and sinister and chilly, but her feet hit some sticky mud quite quickly. To drown herself properly, Miss Spinks would have had to stand on her head, and her grief for Krok made her too tired.

She paddled about for a while, thinking sad thoughts. How would she discipline Flossie without the Viking? Who would keep Cyril in order? *I will do my duty, of course,* thought Miss Spinks miserably, but memories of the Viking kept returning: the way the wood lice clustered in his beard, the way his full belly quivered so manfully beneath his shirt. . . .

She was still thinking these unhappy thoughts when her webbed foot came against something. Something that felt slimy . . . and sort of floating . . . and quite definitely nasty. Telling herself to be brave, she groped in the water to see what it could be.

Miss Spinks gave a squeak and withdrew her hand. It could not have been—but it was—a leg. A human leg! A second leg, also slimy and nasty and almost trouserless, seemed to be beside the first. And a waterlogged and most unpleasant voice said: "Glug!"

It was Oscar the Hulk. He was not dead.

And if he was not dead, then Krok had not killed him. And if Krok had not killed him, he was still under his curse and had no right to be in Valhalla.

Joy exploded inside Miss Spinks like a firecracker.

"Stop glugging," she said to Oscar. "I'll see to you later."

She swooped up the mine shaft like a rocket, roared past the roof of the cinema, and rose up, up into the sky.

A governess with webbed feet couldn't have hoped to catch up with an eight-legged horse. But you can't weigh as much as a small hippopotamus and not need a lot of food, and the Valkyrie had dismounted and was having a snack: a pig's foot that she had taken from her saddlebag and was crunching up noisily between her teeth.

A cry of "Stop! Stop!" in the distance made Krok turn with a sudden hope, and presently Miss Spinks came panting up to them. "A mistake . . . has been made," she gasped—and explained.

The Valkyrie's cheeks puffed out with rage. She snorted. She spat out a mouthful of gristle—but she did not argue, for she knew perfectly well that a mistake had been made. It was she herself who had made it. When you have ninety-nine sisters all pushing and shoving and grabbing at the heroes, the thought of a hero all for yourself is very tempting. Looking out of Valhalla, the Valkyrie had seen Krok push Oscar into the pool and waited no longer before she rushed off to tell Odin that another warrior was on his way.

"Pshaw!" she said furiously. "Verflucht! Yok!"

Then she jabbed Krok for the last time in the stomach, spat once more, and rode away, cursing as she went.

Krok and Miss Spinks were left alone.

"Lettice?" said the Viking, and wondered why he had ever thought it was a silly name. It was a *nice* name—and anyway, what was *wrong* with salad? "Lettice!" he said once more.

Then he moved forward and took the dripping specter in his arms.

LADY TROTTLE WAS preparing for an evening in front of her television set. She had had a lot of trouble lately. Sir Ian had told her that they could no longer go on living at Dunloon, it was too expensive, and this, of course, was dreadfully sad.

But the program she was going to watch had been advertised as the most exciting ever to be televised, and she was looking forward to it very much. She had put on her dressing gown and opened a box of chocolates with squashy middles and told everyone that she was not to be disturbed.

Lady Trottle, though, was not alone. Sitting on the sofa behind her were the Green Lady, the Red Lady, and Headless Hal. They were the sort of ghosts who really don't know what to do with themselves, and they had taken to watching everything, however stupid, on TV.

You could tell how important the program was because the man who came on to announce it was Lionel Twitterstone, who had been knighted by the queen and who usually only covered things like the Grand National or a coronation or a royal tour.

"Ladies and gentlemen," said Sir Lionel, "tonight we bring you one of the great events of television history. Live from the United States by satellite, we bring you— a wedding! But not any wedding! Oh, no! A wedding between two of the most famous characters in America, if not the world: the ghosts of Carra Castle!"

Sir Lionel took a drink of water and Lady Trottle nodded in a pleased way. Alex had telephoned her from Granite Falls and she knew what was coming, but on the sofa, the Ladies and Headless Hal hissed with fury and surprise. What was all this?

"There can scarcely be anyone who has not heard of the heroic rescue by these remarkable spooks of winsome Helen Hopgood, daughter of Hiram C. Hopgood, the multimillionaire."

A picture of Helen now appeared on the screen, and Sir Lionel went on to tell the whole story of Carra Castle, the ghosts' journey to America, their haunting of the cinema, and the adventures that had followed, while on the sofa, the Ladies and Hal gnashed their teeth in rage. Haunting a pigsty, indeed! The wretched outcasts seemed to have done very well for themselves!

"Thrown together by the danger they faced," Sir Lionel went on, "love blossomed between the spirit of a Victorian governess, Lettice Amelia Spinks, and the ghost of a Viking warrior, Krok Fullbelly, who passed on in the year eight hundred and ninety-eight. Ladies and gentlemen, viewers of the world, it is with great pride that we present the first ever spook wedding to be shown on television."

Sir Lionel now looked anxious, but after a short time Carra Castle appeared, covered in flags and bunting.

"Now, while we wait to go into the banqueting hall where the ceremony is to take place, we'll just have a few words with Bernard Potterton, whose brand-new microchemical process has enabled the ectoplasm of ghosts to show up on film."

The words he had with Bernard Potterton were few indeed. The inventor was cut off in the middle of trying to say tri-ethyl-hexo-something-or-other, and the banqueting hall of the castle appeared. A table had been set up with a black cloth and candles, and beside it stood a wizard called Hector Stringer who had come specially from Minnesota to perform the wedding.

The camera moved along the row of guests, picking out Mr. Hopgood, then Helen, then Alex . . .

"And next to the courageous laird of Carra," said Sir Lionel excitedly, "or rather, sitting at his feet—and now please watch very carefully because this animal is the first—the very first real, genuine phantom ever to show up on TV—the hellhound known as Cyril!"

A close-up of Cyril now flashed on to the screen. He looked surprised, twitched an ear—then gave a gigantic yawn.

"Isn't that an appealing face?" cried Sir Lionel. "No wonder this amazing phantom dog, along with the other ghosts, has been signed up by a Hollywood company to make a series of spook movies!"

"Can you believe it?" hissed the Green Lady. "That creature is to become a film star!"

"But now the ceremony is about to begin," Sir Lionel went on, "and here—yes, as clear as daylight, thanks to the Potterton process—is the bridegroom, Krok Full-belly, as he stands waiting for his bride. Have you ever seen a handsomer groom? And beside him, a most un-usual best man: a severed hand!"

The camera moved down to show the Hand, which was holding the ring crooked in its little finger and get-ting ready to climb up the Viking's breeches and give it to him at exactly the right time.

Next there came the most stirring music—the "Lament for the Dead" played on the bagpipes—and the bride entered the hall.

She came on the arm of Uncle Louse, and the old vampire was not in his wheelchair, he was walking! Finding a pair of teeth had changed Uncle Louse from a pathetic creature whose head looked as though it would fall off his withered neck to a strong and upright man. It wasn't the blood he'd had from Ratty Banks, it was knowing that he could be useful; that he *mattered*.

"Whoops!" Sir Lionel had struck a slight snag over the bridesmaid. Flossie wore a wreath of deadly nightshade over her curls and looked a picture, but she'd gotten a bit bored hanging around while Miss Spinks got dressed, and now Hector Springer's spectacles jumped off his nose and started flying around the hall like a mad insect.

But the bride bent down and said a few quiet words, and almost at once the glasses landed back on the wizard's nose. Then she straightened the veil of cobwebs on her freshly drowned hair, and very solemnly and proudly she walked up the aisle to where Krok Fullbelly stood, waiting for her to come.

"Oh, how beautiful! How absolutely beautiful!" Lady Trottle was quite overcome. "Dear, dear Alex, that sweet little girl and those lovely, lovely ghosts! Oh, I do

like a good wedding," she said, turning off the TV and leaning back in her chair.

But the spooks of Dunloon were nearly off their heads with jealousy and fury.

"The show-offs!"

"The sneaky, underhand creeps!"

"How *dare* they!"

"Please be quiet," said Lady Trottle, who was getting a bit fed up with her ghosts. "If you can't behave yourselves, you can go and watch television with the housekeeper."

At this point, Sir Ian Throttle came into the room. He looked serious, as though he had important news, and indeed he had.

"I have found someone to buy Dunloon," he said to his wife. "A very rich American."

On the sofa, the ghosts looked at one another. A very rich American! That meant that Dunloon would be pulled down and shipped across the sea like Carra! And that they, too, would appear on television and become famous film stars!

"We'll show them," said the Green Lady, whirring away with her fan. "We'll be *much* more famous than they are!"

Little did she know what was really going to happen to Dunloon!

NOT LONG AFTER Helen's rescue, the crooks were brought to trial. Oscar was so waterlogged he had to travel on a stretcher, and Ratty was quite crazy, still barking like a dog and telling everyone he had rabies. All of them were found guilty, of course. Oscar got life imprisonment, and Ratty was sent to a special jail for people who weren't just wicked but mad.

But what happened to Adolfa was worse than that.

When they took her to prison, they made her take off her own clothes and put on a prison uniform. Then they took away her locket. Adolfa had been staring into space like a zombie ever since the Hand had frozen her, but now she screamed, rushed forward, and grabbed the locket from the prison wardress. Next she tore it open, and before anyone could stop her, she had taken out Hitler's curls and stuffed them into her mouth.

For a few moments, she chewed at the greasy strands—
then, with a great gulp, she tried to swallow them.

What followed was truly horrible. She coughed. She
spluttered. Her face turned blue . . . then black; she
struggled for breath. Then she fell to the ground,
twitched—and lay still.

Hitler's curl had choked her. Adolfa Batters was dead.

Back in Granite Falls, Mr. Hopgood kept his word. He
gave the castle to the people of the town, and there were
dances and parties to celebrate. As for the Rex Cinema,
it was renamed Spook Palace and became the most famous cinema in the world.

The winter was a busy one. While the ghosts starred
in a film of the Hopgood kidnap, Mr. Hopgood sold his
oil wells and his department stores and his factories and
saw to it that the money he was giving away would be
well spent in helping people all over the world who were
homeless or hungry or poor.

Then, in the late spring, they all sailed back on the
Queen Anne and settled on the beautiful island of Sethsay. Mr. Hopgood had some extra rooms built onto the
old farmhouse, and Aunt Geraldine came to visit and
play bridge with him, which he liked. The school at Errenrig had been closed because there weren't enough

pupils, and the headmaster moved into one of the cottages on the island so that he could teach Helen and Alex, and this worked out very well.

Being back in Scotland was a great joy to the ghosts. Mrs. Fullbelly turned out to be the best wife Krok could have wished for. She never tried to clean out his ears, and because she was so happy her Water Madness got much better, so that for days on end she was almost dry. The Hand had become an author and was writing the story of his life, but once a week Alex rowed him over to the site of the castle, and there, all day, the Hand signed autographs. Carra Point now belonged to the National Trust, and he and the ghosts had become so famous that people came from far and wide to see them.

On a beautiful autumn morning about nine months after Helen's rescue, something unexpected happened. Alex and Helen were throwing sticks for Cyril, who had become rather plump when he was being a film star and needed exercise. Uncle Louse was sunbathing, and Flossie was sitting on a rock singing songs to make the Big Blob come out of the sea and speak to her.

"Good heavens," said Alex, looking up at the sky. "What on earth are those things?"

The others followed his gaze and saw three utterly bedraggled spooks flying wearily over the water. They were so tired that they landed half in the sea, and it was some time before the other ghosts realized who they were.

"Why, if it isn't the Green Lady and the Red Lady and Headless Hal," said Uncle Louse.

The Dunloon ghosts were in a most sorry state. Their grand clothes were crumpled, they had black bruises on their ectoplasm, the Red Lady's hat had been knocked sideways.

Alex looked at them sternly. He knew how unkind they had been to his ghosts, and he wasn't at all pleased to see them.

"What brings you here?" he asked, frowning.

"We're refugees," said the Red Lady. "Outcasts. On the run."

"We're in a terrible state," said the Green Lady.

"We wondered if you could find a corner for us here. Anywhere would do," said Headless Hal. The conceited fop was a wreck, his ruffles torn, his snuffbox lost.

Then they explained what had happened at Dunloon. The rich American who had bought the house had *not* pulled it down and shipped it to America as the ghosts had hoped. He had turned it into a school.

"But not a proper school where children sit at desks and do lessons," said the Green Lady, fanning herself with the few bits of broken tortoiseshell that were left in her fan. "Something called a *progressive* school."

"It's a school where children do exactly what they like and stand on the desks and throw things at the teachers," explained the Red Lady.

The children in the school had been incredibly cruel to the ghosts, putting down banana skins in the corridors and catapulting their ectoplasm, and at last the spooks could take no more.

"We would be grateful for anywhere to haunt—absolutely *anywhere*," said the Green Lady.

But Alex was still angry. "After the way you've behaved, I don't at all see why I should let you live on Sethsay."

Helen, with her kind heart, couldn't help being sorry for the poor, tattered creatures from Dunloon. "Why don't you ask your ghosts what they think?" she said to Alex.

So he did, and his ghosts behaved beautifully. "We'll let bygones be bygones," said Uncle Louse, and Krok said something uplifting in Viking about forgiving those who have done you wrong.

"There's a ruined boat shed on the other side of the island," said Alex. "You can live there, but don't come near us until you have learned to be useful and simple spooks."

So the Dunloon ghosts glided away, and the children made their way back to the house for lunch.

"Are you coming, Flossie?" Helen called as they passed the poltergeist still sitting and singing on her rock.

Flossie shook her head. "I'm waiting for the Big Blob," she said, for she had learned to talk properly at last.

"I do wish he'd come," said Helen to Alex. "The Blob, I mean. I hate to see her just waiting and waiting."

"Then you're silly to wish it," said Alex, "because waiting for things is lovely. The best part, perhaps."

"Like us waiting to go to Patagonia, you mean?"

"Yes, like that."

So they left Flossie on her rock and went back to the house—and to the beautiful smell of sizzling sausages. Mr. Hopgood could eat anything now that he wasn't a millionaire, and the Hand—once you lifted him up to the frying pan—was a fantastic cook!